Ghosts, Vampires, and Werewolves
❖ Eerie Tales from Transylvania ❖

❖ by Mihai I. Spariosu and Dezsö Benedek ❖
❖ illustrated by Laszlo Kubinyi ❖

Orchard Books/New York

For Diana, Eun, Aniko, and Pali
—M.I.S. and D.B.

To the memory of my aunt and uncle,
Eleanora Buchla and Julius Kubinyi
—L.K.

Text copyright © 1994 by Mihai I. Spariosu and Dezső Benedek
Illustrations copyright © 1994 by Laszlo Kubinyi

Orchard Books
95 Madison Avenue
New York, NY 10016

Manufactured in the United States of America
Book design by Rosanne Kakos-Main

10 9 8 7 6 5 4 3 2 1

The text of this book is set in 11 point Novarese Book.
The illustrations are rendered in pen-and-ink.

Library of Congress Cataloging-in-Publication Data

Spariosu, Mihai I.
    Ghosts, vampires, and werewolves : eerie tales from Transylvania /
[retold] by Mihai I. Spariosu and Dezső Benedek ; illustrated by Laszlo
Kubinyi.
        p.   cm.
    Includes bibliographical references.
    Summary: Includes sixteen tales from Transylvanian folklore,
arranged in three sections: Ghosts, Vampires, and Werewolves;
Haunted Treasures; and Eerie Fairy Tales.
    ISBN 0-531-06860-9. — ISBN 0-531-08710-7 (lib. bdg.)
    1. Tales—Romania—Transylvania. [1. Folklore—Romania—
Transylvania. 2. Supernatural—Folklore.] I. Benedek, Dezső.
II. Kubinyi, Laszlo, date, ill. III. Title.
PZ8.1.S729Gh   1994
[398.2'09498]—dc20
                                                                    93-48837

Contents

Acknowledgments

Our debts are many, and it would be impossible to list them all here. We are particularly grateful to Bob Croft, Dan Bradi, Hyangsoon Yi, and Lee Galda Pellegrini of the University of Georgia for their invaluable editorial suggestions; to Ion Cuceu, director of the Institute of Folklore, Liviu Ursuţiu, director of the Library of the Romanian Academy in Cluj-Napoca, Romania, and Father Wilhelm Georg for greatly facilitating our research on the ethnographic background of the stories; to Diana Santiago, Eun Geun, Carola Sautter, Ron Bogue, Stanley Corngold, Frank and Stephanie Chalona, Clea Koré, David Fairchild, Anna Pellegrini, Maria Derevenco, and Giuseppe Mazzotta for reading various drafts of the book and giving us their friendly advice and support; to Nina Jaffe of the Bank Street College of Education, New York, for her excellent comments on the manuscript; and above all to Harold Underdown of Orchard Books for his wonderfully generous editorial help and his unflagging faith in and loyal support of this project. —M.I.S. and D.B.

My thanks to my cousin Muki Kubinyi and to Laszlo Berkovits for their valuable research assistance. —L.K.

Introduction

IN THE NORTH AMERICAN IMAGINATION Transylvania is an eerie land populated by werewolves and vampires, among whom the most famous is Dracula. The Irish writer Bram Stoker based his terrifying character on the legendary figure of Vlad Dracul, a fifteenth-century Wallachian prince (ruled 1456–1462 and 1476–1477), who spent the last part of his life under house arrest in a Transylvanian city. There are many folktales about Vlad Dracul, also known as Vlad the Impaler, but none concerns vampires. Bram Stoker invented his connection with vampirism. However, there is a rich local tradition of ghost, vampire, and werewolf tales in Transylvania. We have drawn upon this folklore in composing our stories, borrowing traditional themes and motifs and recombining them in a personal way. In this we have followed the age-old practice of storytelling, in which storytellers repeat a tale they have heard from their elders, reworking it in the process to suit their own circumstances and the demands of their audience.

We heard many stories while growing up in the Transylvanian mountains. In those days the mountain people lived off the land, farming, raising cattle, hunting, and fishing. They also mined for gold, or panned for it in swift mountain streams. This was not an easy life, so we children had to help our elders with the daily chores. After school we herded animals, fed the fowls in the yard and the cattle in the barn, milked the cows, and watered the horses. We worked in the fields side by side with the grown-ups, making hay or reaping wheat, corn, rye, and barley. We might take grain to be ground at the water mill in the valley or cut trees and gather firewood with our elders in the forest.

After the day's work was done, however, we would have a warm, hearty meal and, especially in winter, gather around a bright fire, children and adults alike. While the old women were busying themselves with carding and spinning wool, they would tell us stories about just or unjust rulers, famous outlaws and bandits, buried treasures, and evil wolves. They would also spin scary yarns about ghosts, vampires, and other restless souls that haunted equally the castles of the rich and the hovels of the poor.

During these exciting evenings of storytelling, the mysterious world of night creatures would come alive in our imaginations, so that we were afraid to venture out alone in the dark. In fact, adults as much as children believed in all kinds of spirits and were careful to protect themselves from the unclean. Our grandmothers would hang wreaths of garlic on the walls, almost everyone wore a cross, and some people would even nail dead bats onto their barn doors, to keep the evil spirits away.

Mountain people were also devoted Christians, and many of their tales show a strong sense of right and wrong based on their Christian beliefs. Christian symbols and rituals like the cross and using holy water come into the stories for another reason: Transylvania, a predominantly Christian principality, was in constant conflict with the neighboring Ottoman Empire, which was predominantly Muslim. In the folk imagination, the Ottoman invaders often appeared as dark, evil forces—vampires or "dark strangers"— while the defenders of Christendom were often presented as the powers of light, goodness, and justice. Through the use of symbolic elements, the tales therefore sometimes play out this political and religious conflict, as often happens when cultures clash.

The great ethnic diversity of Transylvanian mountain people is reflected in their folklore. Transylvania at one time belonged to the Austrian-Hungarian Empire and is now part of Romania. Consequently it is inhabited by a variety of ethnic groups, including Romanians, Hungarians, Germans, Jews, Slovaks, Ukrainians, and Gypsies. Our own family backgrounds show this ethnic diversity. One of us comes from a largely Romanian ethnic background; the other, from a Hungarian one. Like most Transylvanians, however, we are familiar with the main languages spoken in the area and have heard or read many folktales from different groups. We have always been struck by the great number of stories that the various ethnic groups have in common, despite their differences in customs, religious faith, food, clothing, and architecture. Our tales exhibit this mixture of the various ethnic traditions of storytelling in Transylvania, revealing their common human values and concerns.

You will also notice a peculiar blend of irony and humor in these stories, found in even the most gruesome. Historically, this humorous and ironic bent may be a reaction to the very violent and troubled history of the region. Laughter, irony, and sarcasm were ways in which the Transylvanian people attempted to deal with poverty, injustice, social or ethnic conflict, and foreign invasions. Amid all of these natural and man-made disasters, the Transylvanian folk lost neither their hope nor their sense of humor.

We have loosely grouped the stories into three sections. The first, "Ghosts, Vampires, and Werewolves," introduces some of the ghosts and spirits that populate Transylvanian folktales. "Haunted Treasures" concentrates on the spirits that Transylvanian people believe guard the fabulous treasures said to be buried under the ancient ruins scattered all over the land. Transylvania has been famed for its rich gold mines ever since antiquity, when it was a Roman province. The ancient Romans transported immense quantities of gold back to Rome on the *Via Aurea* (the Golden Highway). So we have also included several tales and legends that sprang up about these gold mines and their guardian spirits. The last section, "Eerie Fairy Tales," features stories that combine familiar fairy-tale elements—princesses, castles, and magic beings and objects—with characteristically Transylvanian ones—gruesome endings and black humor.

We believe that readers will enjoy these tales with no further background knowledge. Readers who want to know more may turn to "About the Stories" at the back of the book, where we reveal the source and general background of each story; also, certain words and phrases in some stories are marked with an asterisk (*), meaning there is specific information about them in the back. We do not provide information on everything, of course, because there are things that just can't be explained. . . .

PART ONE
Ghosts, Vampires, and Werewolves

⊰ The White Cross ⊱

Not so long ago there lived a rich farmer who was blessed with all the bounties of this world. He was also blessed with a faithful and loving wife who gave him three sons and one daughter, the likes of whom you could not find in the whole land. In short, this man and his wife were the happiest pair on earth.

But, alas, wise folks know that happiness is a passing shadow in this valley of tears. Unexpectedly the rich man fell ill and died. His grief-stricken widow gave him a proper burial and mourned him for a whole year, according to the ancient custom.

Sorrow was never to leave the poor widow's house. She was still mourning her husband, laying fresh flowers on his grave every day and spending more time with the dead than with the living, when the eldest son passed away, too, followed by the middle one shortly thereafter. She was now left with only her youngest son, Joseph, the apple of her eye, and her little daughter, Anna.

Joseph grew into a strong and handsome youth, while Anna blossomed into a beautiful young maiden. The widow's children were hard-working and obedient, but they brought her little consolation. She spent most of her days in the graveyard, praying by the headstones of her husband and two sons.

When the time came for Joseph to look for a wife, he soon gave up on account of his mother, who could not endure the thought of being left alone when he went courting. For her part, Anna turned away countless suitors, but they kept coming back, for she was not only beautiful and prudent but also well-to-do.

The widow, like all mothers, wanted only what was best for her daughter, despite her fear of losing her. But she could always find some fault with Anna's suitors. This one was not handsome enough, the next not rich enough, and when the lad was both rich and handsome, she would complain that he lived too far away from their village. Time went by, and Anna remained unwed. The widow still spent her days in the graveyard, grieving over her lost husband and sons.

One day, while tending to the graves of her loved ones, the widow cried herself to sleep by her husband's tombstone. And in her sleep she had a dream. She was in a thick, dark forest all alone, wandering through an endless maze of trees, crying out for help, now to her husband, now to her sons, now to her daughter. But no one came. The widow woke up from this fearful premonition and hurried back home.

And sure enough, what did she find in the courtyard but a new suitor more handsome than all the rest, radiant like the sun, strong like an oak, and richly dressed like a king. Anna and her brother took to him immediately, and the widow herself could at first find no fault with him. But then she asked him if he lived far away from their village. "It took me twenty-seven days to ride to your valley," answered the youth, "after crossing the great water."

The poor widow froze. She ached again with the woe of losing her husband and two sons. And now it seemed her daughter was about to marry a foreigner and leave her for good.

"Have pity on me, my dear children," pleaded the widow. "Isn't it enough that death robbed me of your father and brothers? Must I also part from my only daughter, the solace of my old age?"

Joseph, seeing that his sister was torn between filial love and her tender feelings for the youth, spoke up. "Mother dear, perhaps it is the fate of our family to be forever separated. Anna seems to like this suitor best of all and won't part from him easily. Let them be married, and I will make a solemn pledge that whenever your heart yearns for her, I'll bring her back to you, day or night, without fail."

After many such entreaties from her son, the widow gave her blessing to the young couple, and the wedding was celebrated as it can be only in fairy tales. Then the newlyweds bade farewell to Joseph and the weeping mother, and went to live on the bridegroom's estate.

Shortly thereafter, Joseph, the widow's youngest son, the apple of her eye, the one whom she loved best of all, took ill like his father and passed away. The unfortunate mother was beside herself, almost out of her mind with grief. Him she did not bury in the graveyard among the dead but in the garden underneath her bedroom window. She buried him there neither to mourn for him nor to pray for his eternal rest but to curse him day and night:

"Joseph, my loved one, my youngest son, the apple of my eye, come out of your grave and fetch your sister for me. Isn't this what you promised, that you'd bring her without fail? Go now, or I shall curse you to find no rest, for you've robbed me of mine. Rise, my son, or I shall dig you out and curse you for eternity. Let the earth give you no peace, for you've given me none."

And Joseph, finding no peace in his grave because of his mother's wailing and cursing, rose one night and said, "You, dear grave, turn into a horse, and you, dear shroud, turn into a path from here to my sister's house. I must bring her back to Mother, or she'll never let my soul rest in peace."

And at his command his grave turned into a fiery horse, and Joseph mounted him, and his shroud turned into a long, shining path from his mother's house to his sister's. In the twinkling of an eye he flew to Anna's castle, for he rode faster than the wind, at the speed of thought. He had become a *zmeu,** one of the undead.

Anna had not yet gone to bed when Joseph arrived and said, "Sister, dear sister, our mother is longing for you."

"Welcome to my house, brother dear," Anna answered. "But won't you lie down and rest until the morning?"

"I can't rest, sister dear. Come, let's make haste, for we don't want to keep Mother waiting."

Anna did not hesitate. She immediately ordered her carriage and horses, and they set off without delay.

The horses flew as if bewitched, and no wonder, for they were riding along the enchanted path that Joseph's shroud had laid across the land and sea. But the true wonder came before the stroke of midnight, when the birds woke up and sang as loudly as they could: "What sort of earthly order is this, where the living ride together with the dead?"

And the trees, bushes, and grass, and then all the fishes, the whales, and the dolphins of the sea awoke also, shouting after them, "Since when do the living ride with the dead?"

Anna, hearing all these strange voices, could not make them out and asked her brother what they meant.

"Oh, pay no attention to them, sister dear," Joseph reassured her. "They don't know what they are saying."

Once near their mother's house, Joseph asked his sister to wait for him to open the gates. But after he opened them, he heard the cock crow, so he went to lie down in his grave.

Anna waited and waited, but when she realized that her brother was not coming back, she drove her carriage into the courtyard. There she saw an old woman in mourning. Mistaking her black habit for a nun's, she asked, "Holy sister, what are you doing in our yard in the middle of the night?"

"Oh, daughter dear," said the woman, "don't you know your own mother? I am no nun but am mourning Joseph, your brother, who is dead and buried here in the garden, under my bedroom window, so I can curse him night and day for having taken you away from me."

"How can that be, mother dear," cried Anna, "for I've traveled with him all night, till the cock's first crow? He said your heart was longing for me: that's why we made such haste. Oh, God have mercy on me. I've been traveling with a ghoul, an ogre, a *zmeu!*" With these dreadful words, Anna fell dead at her mother's feet.

Overcome by grief, the widow soon breathed her last. With no heirs the family's riches wasted away. The proud manor house fell into disrepair and became inhabited by vermin. The courtyard and the garden were overgrown with weeds and tall grass. In time the wind and the rain did their work, too, erasing the last traces of the ill-fated family, except

for Joseph's grave. There the village folks placed a white wooden cross, to quiet Joseph in his resting place.

Travelers who pass by that white cross on a moonlit night may still see an old woman dressed in a nun's black habit, wandering around the meadow and wailing, "Joseph, my loved one, my youngest son, the apple of my eye, come out of your grave and fetch your sister for me. Rise, my son, or I shall dig you out and curse you for eternity. Let the earth give you no peace, for you've given me none."

⇥ The Forest ⇥

ONCE THERE WAS a crew of woodcutters who worked in the huge Transylvanian forest. They felled trees and rolled the logs down the steep slopes, pushing them into a swift and treacherous mountain river. The river took the logs racing through the valleys to a lumberyard many miles away.

The men had almost cleared one slope of a tall mountain. Only a small patch of forest remained, so the crew got together to decide what to do next. As they sat down around an open fire, the eldest among them, a man called Mathias, took out a bottle of plum brandy. First the old man poured a few drops of brandy on the ground. "Here, this is for you," the old woodcutter said, addressing the spirits of the forest* with respect. "Please don't harm us."

Then Mathias drank from the bottle and passed it on to the others. After each man had taken a hearty swig, the last one handed the bottle back to Mathias. With a few drops left at the bottom of the bottle, the old man turned again toward the forest and poured the remaining brandy on the ground. "Look, we're giving you the last drop. Please spare us," he implored the spirits.

Now that the bottle was finished, the old man addressed his companions. "We've been working on this mountain for almost a year," he said, "and so far we've been spared any serious trouble. But you know that when their forest is cut, the spirits often demand a man's life. We must be careful and follow the old customs to get out of here safely. Tomorrow is our last day, so let's leave the last patch of forest untouched. Otherwise, you never know what the ancient ghosts may do to us."

9

Among those sitting around the fire was a man called Jakob, with his two sons, Martin and Michael.

"Oh, stop boring us with your old wives' tales, Mathias," said Jakob. "No one believes in that stuff anymore. Why not finish our job properly and earn another day's pay? My sons and I will get up at daybreak as usual, do our share of work, and get out of here before noon. The rest of you can do as you please." With these words Jakob and his two sons stood up and walked back to the log cabin. Soon afterward they were sound asleep.

The others remained sitting quietly around the fire. Those who knew the forest well shared Mathias's worries. Those who were young and inexperienced did not know whom or what to believe. The uneasy silence was broken only by the plaintive hoot of an owl coming from the direction of the cabin. "I hope this will end well," said old Mathias, shaking his head, and then he stood up. The men put out the fire and retired to the cabin for the night.

At dawn, while the rest of the crew was still asleep, Jakob and his two sons set to work. The mountain echoed with the heavy blows of their axes, and within a few hours they had felled several trees. By the time the rest of the crew rousted themselves out of the cabin, Jakob and his sons had nearly finished their share of work for the day.

"Get to work, you sluggards," Jakob teased the others. "You've already wasted half the morning."

Most of the men could still not make up their minds whether to cut the rest of the trees or just pick up and leave. Suddenly they heard a chilling scream. As one man, they all ran toward the source of the terrifying sound.

Under a tall black fir, close to the tree's roots, lay Michael, Jakob's younger son. He had stepped into a bear trap. The steel jaws of the huge contraption had snapped shut over his right knee, almost slicing his leg in two. Blood pumped out of the gaping wound, and hard as they tried, the men could not stop the bleeding. In less than ten minutes the lad lay dead in his father's arms.

The men were stunned. Nobody breathed a word about Mathias's warning of the previous night, nor did anyone mention the spirits of the forest. They all remained gathered around the lad's corpse.

Since they were far away from home, Jakob decided to bury his son behind the log cabin. The crew held an overnight wake for him, quiet and orderly but for the sobbing of Jakob. The next morning they performed a simple funeral, marking the boy's resting place with a white birch cross. Old Mathias spoke at the grave. After reading a passage from the Bible, he begged the spirits of the forest to be content with one life and not harm the crew any further.

But the boy's father, blinded by grief and infuriated by the old man's sermon, ran into the cabin and grabbed an oil lamp. Rushing to the edge of the forest, he smashed the lamp against a tree and lit the spilled oil. The tree burst into flames. "Here, forest ghosts," he shrieked. "Take this!" With maddened eyes he stared at the huge flames that quickly engulfed the tree.

The crew stood by helpless, dumbfounded by the enormity of the madman's act. Then a strange thing happened. Although the huge tree was immediately consumed by the wild wind-fanned flames, no other tree caught on fire. With tears in his eyes Mathias thanked the forest spirits under his breath and started back for the cabin to gather his things. He had made up his mind to leave at once. But his crew's ordeal had only begun.

Jakob called his son Martin, and together they started hacking savagely at the trees. Mathias and the rest of the crew rushed forward to restrain them, but suddenly, as if held back by an invisible hand, they stopped dead in their tracks. Unable to move or cry out, they saw a tall, almost transparent figure appear behind Martin.

The eerie apparition touched the lad's right shoulder and then dissolved into thin air. At just that moment Martin's ax recoiled as if it had hit tempered steel, slipping out of the lad's hands and crashing into his forehead. It happened so fast that the unlucky youth could not even cry out. All the crew heard was the dull thump of a cracked skull, and the next instant, Martin lay dead at his father's feet.

Jakob uttered an unearthly moan and, seizing Martin's ax, started attacking something in the air, invisible to the others. He foamed at the mouth, howled, and swung the ax around wildly. After inflicting several wounds upon himself, he rushed past the crew and headed for the river.

Pandemonium broke loose, and the crew, finally able to move, ran after the shrieking madman. But when they reached the riverbank, old Mathias held them back. "Stay where you are," he said, crossing himself. "There's nothing we can do for him now."

As if pursuing an invisible enemy, Jakob splashed through the shallows at the river's edge. He pushed a floating log ahead of him and plunged into the middle of the swift current. Suddenly the huge stack of logs piled up on the riverbank came tumbling into the water, and the stream filled up with hundreds of tree trunks. Bobbing up and down on the foamy waves, the logs started racing down the river, spinning and crashing into one another.

The crew spotted Jakob struggling to hang on to his log. Then a raft appeared out of nowhere behind him, and on it there stood an old man. The frenzied woodcutter also caught sight of the stranger and shouted for help. But the old man paid no attention to the drowning man. In desperation Jakob let the raft float by him, then, grabbing its end, pulled himself onto what he thought would be safety. The old man stood with his back to the intruder and was not in the least affected by the raft's violent heaving and shaking. "Who are you?" screamed Jakob.

The stranger said nothing. The woodcutter started crawling toward him, but his feet got caught between the logs. He tried to stand up, but at that very instant the raft ran under a large tree whose trunk arched over the swift current.

The others watched in disbelief as the huge trunk passed through the stranger as if he were mist and hit Jakob squarely in the chest. There he remained, impaled on the tree branches with the logs rushing underneath him, tearing off his legs. The white foam of the river soon turned red with the blood of the unfortunate soul. The speechless men on the bank could only watch as the raft with its mysterious traveler disappeared into the turbulent waves.

By the next day the rest of the crew had buried Jakob and Martin next to Michael and had finished packing their belongings. They walked away from the cabin without looking back at the three white crosses by the small patch of trees left uncut. All they could think about was the long journey ahead of them through the vast Transylvanian forest.

⇥ The Bitang ⇤

IN A REMOTE HAMLET in the Transylvanian Alps there once dwelt a lonely old woman with her only son, born out of wedlock. The youth was so good-looking that everyone called him Nicholas the Handsome. He could sing and dance well, and he was a fine storyteller. Whenever he attended a wedding or christening, he was sure to turn it into a memorable event. So folks from all over the valley started hiring him to entertain their guests at festive occasions. And since he was so handsome, rarely did he leave a party without someone to share his bed. Gradually the young man's ways became more and more dissolute.

The old woman felt very ashamed of her son's loose conduct. Whenever Nicholas was away, she sat home alone crying quietly. "He's turned out just like his dead father," she would sigh, wiping her tears. And in vain did she beg him to change his ways. The older her son grew, the looser he became, and the rumor even reached her that he had fathered several children. Finally Nicholas's mother could no longer bear her shame and died of a broken heart.

Some years later Nicholas grew tired of feasting and merrymaking and decided to slow down a little. He bought himself a flock of sheep and a small farm at the edge of the forest. He tended his flock all day and made a good living by selling sheep's cheese in the neighboring villages. But he still preferred skirt-chasing to marrying and raising a family.

One crisp winter afternoon Nicholas was coming back from a nearby village. Climbing up a steep ravine, his skis strapped to his back, he thought he saw a dark shadow darting behind the bushes on the hilltop. When he arrived at the spot, he looked around but saw nothing alarm-

14

ing. He put on his skis and continued through the forest. Yet he had an uncanny feeling that someone was following him.

As Nicholas came within sight of his farm, he was relieved and stopped to rest for a minute. Suddenly he felt a sharp blow on the back of his head and fell down in the snow. A fierce growl told him he was being attacked by a wolf.

Luckily the high collar of the coat Nicholas was wearing prevented the beast from breaking his neck, but its sharp fangs tore deep into his skin. Nicholas rolled a few yards down the snowy slope and, shaking his attacker loose, drew his dagger. Blinded by the snow in his eyes, he stabbed wildly at the air around him until he realized the wolf was gone. Then he rose, trembling, to his feet and ran all the way home.

Around midnight Nicholas was still washing his neck wounds with strong camomile tea* when he heard a wolf's howl under his bedroom window. The sheep started to bleat in their pen, and the dog barked furiously. Soon the barking turned into a pitiful yelp, and all became quiet. Nicholas stayed up most of the rest of the night, sick with worry. Finally, just before daybreak, he fell asleep, exhausted.

Stepping out on the porch the next day, Nicholas saw that the snow in his front yard was full of wolf tracks. "There must have been dozens of them," he whispered anxiously, and went to check on his horse and sheep. The farm animals were all right, but near the stable lay his dog's spiked collar in a huge puddle of frozen blood. Horrified, Nicholas picked up the collar and ran back into the house, where he remained for the rest of the day.

The following morning Nicholas had to go to the village again. He tried to bandage his wounded neck by wrapping a piece of cloth around it, but the cloth was too short to be tied together. Looking for something to hold it in place, he came upon the steel-spiked dog collar. This should do nicely, he thought, fitting the collar over his bandage.

The collar's sharp steel spikes made him look so fierce that Nicholas was startled when he glanced at himself in the mirror. Disguising the collar with a thick woolen scarf, he went to the stable to get his horse. Soon he was on his way to the village.

Just before a clearing where there stood the cabin of an old woodcutter and his son, Nicholas's horse spooked, throwing him into a snowbank. A huge gray wolf leaped out of the thick underbrush and, growling savagely, tore into the horse's neck.

Nicholas ran for his life. He pounded desperately on the cabin door and rushed inside as soon as the woodcutter's son opened it for him. Gasping for breath, Nicholas told the son, who was one of his old carousing companions, about the savage beast that had been stalking him relentlessly for two days.

"This is very odd," said Nicholas's friend while putting on his winter coat. "Lone wolves rarely attack humans in broad daylight, and even more rarely so close to their homes." Then he grabbed his gun and filled his pockets with ammunition. "Let's see if we can teach him a lesson."

"Why go out there, son?" said the old woodcutter, who until then had been sitting quietly by the warm brick stove. "This doesn't concern you. Besides, what Nicholas needs is not a shotgun but a priest and holy water. Wasn't he sired by Michael the Handsome? Like father, like son."

Nicholas was about to ask the old woodcutter what he meant by these strange words, but his friend intervened.

"Oh, never mind my old man," said the son. "His head is full of superstitions and silly tales. Let's go and get that wolf of yours."

"In God's name, son, don't leave the house, I beg you."

"Go back to sleep, Father. We'll hear your stories after dinner."

Ignoring the old woodcutter's warning, the two men opened the heavy oak door and stepped onto the porch. The brisk mountain air was filled with the sickly odor of fresh blood, and from the woods nearby there came menacing howls. Shaking like a leaf, Nicholas walked behind the woodcutter's son.

As in a dream, Nicholas saw his former attacker leap out of nowhere and land on top of his friend, bringing him down in the snow. The man's agonizing shriek was cut short as the wolf's fangs tore open his throat. When it was all over, the wolf put its front paws on the corpse and, lifting its bloodstained muzzle toward the sky, howled fiercely. Several other

wolves then rushed out of the woods and started devouring the human flesh.

Nicholas felt he was about to collapse, but he tried to compose himself. Grabbing his friend's gun, he started racing back toward the cabin. Behind him he heard again the leader's horrifying howl, echoed instantly by the whole pack. Nicholas did not have to turn around to know they were now pursuing him. In his haste he neglected to take care with his footing; he slipped and fell on his back, only a few steps away from the cabin.

The lead wolf went for his throat, pressing its jaws past the barrel of the gun. As the beast bit down on his neck, Nicholas could hear its teeth crack on the steel spikes of the dog collar. Its mouth torn to shreds, the wolf recoiled.

Still on his back, Nicholas fired both barrels of the shotgun at his attacker. The blast caught the wolf in the chest and threw it back into the other charging beasts. Nicholas rose to his feet and ran to the cabin door.

"Let me in," he screamed, banging his fists on the door.

"Go away, you murderer," said the old man inside.

"Help me!" Nicholas shrieked. "Help me—let me in!"

"Why don't you ask them for help? Just look behind you."

Nicholas cast a quick glance behind him and froze. The wolves had moved back a few yards, and, huddled in the snow, there lay a human form. Nicholas felt as though he were losing his mind.

"What's all this about, old man?" he shouted through the door. "What's going on?"

"Only wretched sinners like you forget that a seventh son born out of wedlock joins the unclean and turns into a wolf," said the old man inside.

"What?" whispered Nicholas.

"Go look at him. He's much like yourself, for he's a *bitang*,* one of your bastard sons."

Nicholas felt rage and fear billowing inside him. He started kicking the cabin door as hard as he could.

"Old man, you're mad. Let me in before they tear me to pieces."

"I wish they would. But they rarely harm one of their own. Now go away before I shoot you."

Overwhelmed, Nicholas turned around and staggered over to the corpse in the snow. It had been a slender, handsome youth, but now his lips were torn and bloody, his chest carved open by the gun blast. Nicholas gazed into the lad's cloudy eyes and there, giving him unbearable pain, he discovered his own young image. Sobbing, he fell to his knees and bent over the lifeless boy.

"Go away, *bitang*! You are cursed." Nicholas heard the old man's angry voice. The door opened slightly, and a bullet whizzed past him.

Filled with shame and remorse, Nicholas tried to stand up, but he could not. He tried again, but dropped back in the snow on all fours. With horror he saw that his arms were now covered with dark gray fur. Before his very eyes his hands shriveled up and changed into paws.

The dog collar grew tight and stifling around his stiffening, thick neck. As he tried to shake it loose, its clasp snapped, and the collar fell into the snow. Letting out a long howl, he disappeared into the forest, followed by his pack of wolves.

⊹ The Jealous Vampire ⊹

ONCE IN A VILLAGE there lived a wise old woman. On long winter nights young maidens would gather at her house to card wool or do other handiwork together. Sometimes young men would also drop by, to court and make merry with them.

The most beautiful maiden of all, the daughter of a wealthy man to boot, kept aloof from the lads. Then one day a handsome stranger came by, and she was swept off her feet. She allowed him to take her into his arms and kiss her. But when the cock crowed for midnight, he vanished without a trace.

"Maria, my girl," said the old woman, who had watched the stranger all evening, "did you notice anything unusual about your young man?"

"What should I notice, auntie dear?"

"Unless I'm mistaken, your beau had rooster's feet."

"Goodness gracious, auntie, I never noticed anything like that," said Maria. But the girl worried nevertheless and promised herself to take a good look at her beau's feet next time.

The handsome stranger came back again the following evening. He fondled and kissed Maria till midnight. Then the cock crowed, and the lad disappeared.

This time the old woman had noticed that the stranger had horse's hooves for feet. But Maria had seen nothing unusual, even though she had looked at him carefully. She went home, rose early, and did her share of the household chores. In the evening she again took her distaff and went back to the old woman's house.

When her beau appeared, Maria was ready for him. Without the lad noticing it, she stuck a threaded needle into the back of his coat. As before, he went away when the cock crowed, and no one knew where he had gone.

At daybreak Maria followed the trail of her thread, which ran from the old woman's house all the way to the graveyard. There she found her beau all rotten and covered with worms, lying in a ditch outside the graveyard fence. Scared out of her wits, the girl ran to the wise old woman who had seen through the vampire* from the outset. She received the maiden very kindly and told her how to deal with him. Maria felt a little better and promised to follow the old woman's advice faithfully, no matter how much pain it might cause her.

Not long before the stroke of midnight, who should come to Maria's house but her beau from the ditch. He had first gone to the old woman's, had not found his sweetheart there, and so came knocking at Maria's window.

"Are you home, my bride?" he whispered. "What did you see this morning on the way to the graveyard? Maria, answer me or I'll kill your father."

"I didn't see anything," replied the maiden.

The lad grew very angry. He walked noiselessly into her elders' bed-chamber and strangled Maria's father in his sleep. Then the cock crowed, and the lad returned to his ditch.

A week later he rose with the full moon and knocked again at Maria's window.

"Tell me, my bride," said the youth, "what did you see last week on the way to the graveyard?"

"Nothing," answered Maria.

"Tell me what you saw, or I'll kill your mother."

"I saw nothing," persisted the maiden.

Then the enraged youth strangled her mother as well, and went to lie down in his ditch.

Maria cried and cried, but there was nothing she could do. That after-noon she buried her mother in the churchyard by her father's side, according to custom. Then, remembering the old woman's advice, Maria went home and addressed her servants:

"I have plenty of gold and many oxen and sheep, as you well know. I'm giving them all to you, because I'll die tonight. But if you don't do my bidding, my curse will follow you beyond the grave. Once you find my corpse, make a hole in the wall* and carry me out of the house through it. Then bury me under the old apple tree at the edge of the forest."

The servants started weeping, but they could not have helped her even if they had known what was wrong. So they agreed to do what she asked.

That evening Maria's beau rose again with the full moon and came to her window. "Are you home, my bride?" he asked.

"Yes, I am."

"Tell me, what did you see on the way to the graveyard?"

"I saw nothing."

The youth realized Maria would never obey him, and so he came in through the window and strangled her. Then the cock crowed, and he went to lie down in his ditch.

The next morning Maria's servants found her corpse lying in the bedchamber. They made a hole in the wall and carried her coffin through it. Obeying her last wish, they buried her under the apple tree at the edge of the forest.

Now one day the son of a boyar* happened to go hare-hunting near Maria's village. His greyhounds ran all over the forest until they came upon the girl's grave. And behold, a flower had grown on it, so beautiful and rare that you could not have found its match anywhere in the world. The greyhounds started sniffing and barking around the grave, and then they lay down upon it.

The boyar's son sounded his horn, calling his hounds back, but they would not budge. Riding up to them, the youth noticed the beautiful flower shining like a beacon. He quickly dismounted, pulled out the plant, and took it home with him. After showing the wonder to his parents, he planted it in a flowerpot that he placed at the head of his bed.

At night, while the youth was asleep, the flower came out of its pot and turned into the beautiful maiden. Maria got into bed next to the lad, kissing and biting his neck. After a while she laid her head on his chest and fell asleep in his arms. But the youth just continued sleeping and was none the wiser, for when the cock crowed, the girl turned into a flower again and went back to her pot.

In the morning the lad felt very ill. "My neck and chest are frightfully sore," he complained to his parents. His mother sent for the doctor, but he could find nothing wrong with the boy. Finally the lad dragged himself out of bed and went about his daily business. But in the evening, as soon as he fell asleep, the flower turned into the maiden again, taking him in her arms. At the stroke of midnight Maria returned to her pot, and the next morning the youth awoke feeling even worse than the day before.

And so it went for several nights, until the boyar became worried and told his wife, "There's something strange about that flower, because ever since our son brought it home, he's been constantly ill. Let's keep watch tonight and find out who or what has been harming our boy."

The parents carefully hid in the lad's bedroom, and well before midnight whom should they see leaping out of the flowerpot but a maiden more beautiful than a golden icon. The boyar jumped out of hiding and caught Maria by the hand, thus breaking the vampire's spell that her old beau had put on her.

When the youth woke up and set eyes on Maria, he instantly fell in love with her and asked her to be his bride. The maiden was overjoyed, not only because he was so handsome but also because everything was turning out just as the wise old woman had told her it would. The boyar threw a splendid wedding feast for the young couple, and all the guests were dazzled by the shining beauty of the bride and groom. Before the year was out, Maria gave birth to a golden-haired baby boy, to the great delight of the whole family.

But Maria's old beau got wind of her whereabouts. So one night he came to the boyar's manor house and knocked on her window. "Maria, my unfaithful bride," he called, "what did you see last year on the way to the graveyard?"

"I saw nothing," replied Maria, remembering the old woman's instructions.

"Tell me or I'll kill your little boy."

"I have nothing to tell you," she persisted.

Thereupon the vampire went to the baby's cradle and strangled him.

Maria rose and took the corpse of her little son to the boyar's chapel, hiding it in an empty crypt. The vampire came back the following night and asked her, "Maria, what did you see?"

"I saw nothing."

"Tell me, or I will kill your husband, the boyar's son."

"That you shall not do, or I will pray to God that he strike you dead."

When the vampire saw that Maria cared for her husband more than for anyone else in the world, he became so mad with jealousy that he did not hear the cock crow. Having stayed out past midnight, he began to swell until he blew up, turning to dust.

At daybreak Maria ran to her father-in-law and asked him to tear out his heart as quickly as he could. Without questioning her, the boyar bared his chest, tore out his heart, and laid it in Maria's hands. She took the throbbing heart* to her son's crypt and brought him back to life with the blood dripping from it. Next she hurried to the churchyard where her parents lay buried and let a few drops of blood fall on their graves. And behold, they also rose from the dead.

Quickly Maria returned the throbbing heart to her father-in-law, who put it back in his chest. Then she thanked him, telling him everything that had happened and how the wise old woman had taught her to use the vampire's jealousy in order to get rid of him. The boyar praised her courage and endurance, and they all lived happily ever after.

❧ Special Delivery ❧

IN A SMALL MOUNTAIN TOWN there once lived a postman named Erwin. Each day he would hitch up his old horse to his rickety dogcart and deliver the mail to the families all around. He had been the postman in that town all his life, so he knew practically everything there was to know about everyone in his district—or so he thought.

One late afternoon Erwin had almost finished his deliveries when he discovered a small package in the bottom of his mailbag with a note attached to it. The note was from the postmaster of a remote Transylvanian district and said,

> Dear Colleague,
>
> The other day an old man dressed in rich but tattered clothes burst into our post office, slapped this parcel on the counter, and ordered my junior clerk to send it by special delivery. Because the old man had no money for the postage, my clerk, who is young and inexperienced, laughed in his face. Whereupon the stranger became violently angry, grabbed the clerk by the throat, and screamed, "Who are you to dare disobey my orders? This must be delivered at once, do you hear me, you miserable scoundrel?" No sooner did he utter these words than he started choking, clutched at his heart, and dropped to the floor. By the time I arrived on the scene, he was lifeless. Since he obviously was not from our parts and had given no return address, I am sending the parcel on to you in hopes you can collect the postal fees upon delivery.
>
> Yours sincerely,

To Erwin's surprise, the inscription on the parcel read, "Shadowfield Castle. To be delivered by hand." Of course, he knew where the castle was, a long drive out of town and up the hill. But the distance didn't bother Erwin. No, what bothered him was that the castle had been abandoned for ages, and although he had heard strange rumors about it in his childhood, as far as he knew, no one ever went up there. He had certainly never delivered any mail there before.

"Oh, well, duty comes first," Erwin sighed, and headed his horse and cart up the mountain road.

Everyone he passed wondered where he could be going at that late hour, as Erwin left behind house after house until finally there were no more houses, only the forest and the dark castle perched on the top of a steep hill.

When Erwin reached Shadowfield, he found the front gate shut tight and locked. This did not deter him. He walked along the wall until he discovered a hole large enough to crawl through. The yard was overgrown with weeds so tall that he could barely see the pathway leading to the front door.

He knocked on the door several times, but no one answered, so he began to search for a window to peer through. The place seemed completely deserted, and in the eerie silence the postman could hear every pebble and grain of sand screech under his shoes. Finally he found a broken shutter and looked inside.

He saw a spacious hall filled with cobwebs, old-fashioned furniture covered by dust, and a huge fireplace made of black marble. Nothing strange or especially unusual. "Well, there's no one here to accept this package," he decided. But just as he turned away, he thought he glimpsed a small spark glowing in the fireplace. "It can't be," he said, trying to reassure himself. When he looked back at it, the spark suddenly erupted into a raging flame that filled the whole hall with smoke and soot.

Terrified but still clutching the parcel to his chest, Erwin raced across the yard and through the hole in the garden wall, almost crashing into his dogcart. He jumped in and urged his horse down the hill just as quickly as the old nag could go. After a minute or two Erwin gathered enough courage to glance back at Shadowfield. A huge column of dense, black smoke was billowing out of the castle's largest chimney.

As soon as he reached the town, Erwin went to the house of the chief of police. It did not matter to him that the chief was in the middle of his supper. Erwin burst into the dining room and told him that he had to speak with him at once.

The chief invited the postman into the parlor and offered him a glass of wine. When he heard what had happened back at Shadowfield, the chief shook his head and said, "It's understandable that you are upset. I think, however, that there is someone who can unravel this mystery for us."

The chief left the room for a moment, and when he came back, he explained, "Many years ago there was a terrible tragedy at Shadowfield. Perhaps this parcel is somehow connected with it. I don't know the whole story, but I've sent for Hannes, the castle's old butler. When he gets here, he can tell us what he knows."

In a little while there was a knock, and old Hannes hobbled in with the help of a cane. He was very grotesque-looking. His left eye was misted over with a large cataract, and even worse, his right ear was missing. The host greeted the newcomer, offered him a glass of wine, and then plunged right into the heart of the matter. "What can you tell us about the tragedy at Shadowfield?" he asked.

Hannes shuddered at the mention of the castle's name. At first he acted as if he wished to leave the house without speaking, but then he faced the two men and said, "I haven't spoken to anyone about that accursed castle ever since I left it, but now that I'm growing old, it may be time to share the burden of my secret with someone. So if you'll be patient, I'll explain everything to you." And after sipping absently from his wineglass, the old butler began his tale.

I was a mere boy when I first saw Shadowfield Castle. To me it seemed very beautiful, the most magnificent dwelling I could imagine, for I had been raised on a distant farm in the hills. I worked first as a gardener and later in the kitchen as an assistant to the cook. Then one day I was ordered to start serving the baron his meals. The Master, as everyone called him, was stubborn, coldhearted, and cruel to most people. Any hint of disobedience would throw him into a fit of rage, and he would whip servants and relatives alike without mercy. But for some reason he took a liking to me and soon promoted me to the position of head butler.

The trouble really began when the Master's wife died suddenly, not long after giving birth to their son, Ludwig. In order to forget his grief, the baron traveled abroad frequently and left the raising of his son to relatives. The child grew to be as different from his father as night from day. He was kind, compassionate, and very handsome. When Ludwig turned eighteen, his father finally started showing an interest in him and began to take him along on his journeys.

But on one occasion the Master left Ludwig home, telling his son he would have a surprise for him when he came back. Growing bored, the young nobleman one day decided to accompany me to town to taste the new wines that had been ordered for the baron's wine cellar. When we entered the old marketplace, Ludwig glanced up the street and, as fate would have it, saw a lovely young girl holding a basket of mushrooms. "Mushrooms, fresh mushrooms," the girl called in a voice so melodious and sweet that Ludwig immediately lost his heart to her. He walked up to her and asked, "Where did you find such rare delicacies?"

"In the forest," she replied, blushing at his forwardness. But imagine her surprise when the next words out of his mouth were a proposal of marriage. The young girl responded in jest that she would indeed marry him if he would buy all her mushrooms. Ludwig quickly produced a gold coin sufficient to buy the whole basket ten times over and asked her to deliver the mushrooms to the castle that very afternoon.

Once home, Ludwig sat down by a window, eagerly awaiting the girl's arrival. Finally, after what seemed to him endless hours, he saw her approaching the castle with the basket of mushrooms under her arm. He rushed out to meet her, opening the gate and trying to draw her inside.

But she refused to enter, simply laying down the basket by the gate and turning to leave. Ludwig was afraid that she didn't think he was serious about marrying her, so he asked her to wait one moment while he went into the castle to get something.

When Ludwig returned, he produced a beautiful golden ring set with a magnificent ruby. Taking her hand, he said, "This ring is a family heirloom that belonged to my mother. I want you to have it as a token of my love for you until we can be properly engaged and married." The ring fit perfectly, as if it had been made for the stranger's hand.

The girl blushed with pleasure, becoming even more beautiful in the young man's eyes. He wanted more than anything to take her in his arms, but suddenly, without a word, the girl turned and ran away. It was then that Ludwig realized he did not even know her name.

After searching the countryside with my help, the lovesick youth finally learned that the girl, Erika, lived with her parents on a farm. Ludwig began to visit her every day either at the farm or in the marketplace. Before long it was clear to all of us that Erika had also fallen in love with our handsome young master.

I knew that trouble was coming, though, and I trembled for their safety.

Sure enough, a few days later Ludwig's father returned from his surprise journey. He had been seeking a suitable bride for his son and had succeeded in arranging a marriage to the daughter of one of the richest noblemen in the land. The wedding date was set for six weeks hence.

Stunned, poor Ludwig said nothing about Erika for fear of his father's wrath. But as the weeks passed, his health began to decline so badly that soon even the Master noticed. One day he called Ludwig into his chamber and asked, "What's the matter, my son? Aren't you pleased with the match that I've obtained for you?"

Ludwig could contain himself no longer. "No, Father," he burst out. "I'm the most miserable of all men, for I love another. Her name is Erika. She's a peasant girl, but she's stolen my heart away, and I'll marry none but her."

The Master, not used to being disobeyed, somehow managed to conceal his rage, but later that afternoon he summoned me into his presence and demanded that I tell him what I knew about Erika. I stood trembling yet silent in front of him as he screamed, "How has this peasant so bewitched my son that he'd disobey his own father?" When I made no reply, his anger mounted higher. "What's your part in this plot?" he bellowed. In a flash he drew his dagger and sliced off my right ear, yelling curses at me the whole time.

I was in terrible pain and more frightened than I had ever been, but the worst was yet to come. Removing a whip from the wall, he started cracking it very close to my face. One lash caught my left eyeball, blinding me. I feel certain he would have blinded my other eye as well, but at that moment Ludwig rushed into the room.

"What are you doing, Father?" he exclaimed. "It won't do you any good to kill this poor servant, for I will marry Erika and no one else." The Master, now thoroughly provoked, turned the whip on his son, and it was not long before Ludwig, too, was as bloody as I. Yet, even so, he showed no fear. "You can lash me to death," he bravely challenged his enraged sire. "But if I live, tomorrow morning I will ask Erika's parents for her hand in marriage."

Oddly enough, this open defiance seemed to calm the baron, for suddenly he dropped his whip. "So you want her hand," he repeated quietly, his eyes like steel, his mouth twisted into a savage grin. "Well, her hand you shall have."

Later that day the Master went into town in search of Erika. When someone pointed her out to him in the old marketplace, the baron rode up to the girl and tossed her a gold coin.

"Bring all your mushrooms to Shadowfield at once," he commanded and then departed.

The unsuspecting maiden followed on foot, and once through the castle's main gate, she stopped to rest a little, hoping to catch a glimpse of Ludwig. Instead, his father appeared and ushered her into the great hall.

Inside the hall the Master's eyes fell on Erika's ring. As he recognized it immediately, his rage erupted anew. Before the girl knew what had happened or why, he had drawn his dagger and stabbed her to death.

Then the Master took a sharp sword from the wall and, with one swing, hacked off her hand. Picking up the severed hand, he strode determinedly to Ludwig's room, with the blood of the innocent girl staining the halls as he went.

The Master found us standing near the window, where Ludwig was dressing my damaged eye, comforting me the best he could. "Here," said the baron, hurling the maiden's hand at his son. "That's what you wanted to ask her parents for, wasn't it?"

Recognizing his mother's ring, the youth understood in a flash what his father had done. He screamed and then, backing away from the ghastly sight in horror, crashed through the tall castle window behind him, falling to his death.

That same day Ludwig was laid to rest in the family crypt, and Erika was secretly buried under an old walnut tree behind the castle. Showing no signs of remorse, the baron handed out fistfuls of gold to all the servants to buy their silence. But no amount of gold could match the terror they felt in the presence of their ruthless master, and they began to desert him one by one.

For my part, I had no place to go, so I stayed on. After Ludwig's death, I hardly ever saw the Master. He traveled more and more, and when he did come home, he would never talk to anyone. But one night strange things started happening. A huge flame shot out of the fireplace in the main hall, sending clouds of black smoke all over the castle. I could hear loud footsteps everywhere, but saw no one. Then I heard screams in the baron's bedchamber. The Master flung his door wide open and started running through the smoke-filled halls. "No, you can't have it!" he was shrieking at the top of his lungs. "You won't have it, not till the day I die. Out, get out of my sight!"

I thought he had gone insane, so I took refuge in my room, locking the door behind me. Immediately I had an eerie feeling that I was not alone and looked around me. The moon shone in through the branches of the walnut tree, and in the dim light I saw Ludwig sitting in an armchair near the window. He looked pale and mournful. "Please find her hand," he said to me. "Please give it back to us." Then he faded away, and all I could see was the old walnut tree looming over my window.

Hannes paused a little to draw his breath, and the police chief silently poured more wine into the old man's glass. The butler took a small sip and then shuddered as if the wine had suddenly stirred more dreadful memories within him. But he was now determined to finish his story.

"The next day the Master went away for good," Hannes said. "He took all his gold and belongings and left no instructions for the estate. The few remaining servants had fled the night before, so I was left alone in that gloomy castle. Night after night the same huge flame shot out of the fireplace, and I saw Ludwig's mournful ghost roaming through the hallways and the garden. He would always stop by the old walnut tree outside my window. I began to search all over the castle for Erika's severed hand, but without any luck. I became convinced that the cruel Master had taken it away with him.

"In the end I became so unnerved by Ludwig's nightly visits that I decided to leave. The authorities locked up the estate, and I've never set foot in there since that day. It happened so long ago that now it all seems like a bad dream."

Old Hannes sighed and took another sip of wine. The chief of police and the postman looked at each other in silence as if the same thought had crossed their minds.

"It may seem like a bad dream," said the chief, "but who can doubt the reality of it now? This evening, Erwin tried to deliver a small package to Shadowfield, and when he looked through a window, he saw the same huge flame shooting out of the fireplace that you've just described. It appears that the young baron is still roaming the hallways in search of his bride's hand."

Hannes blanched and crossed himself. "What package did you deliver there, Erwin?" he asked feebly.

"I wasn't able to deliver it," the postman said. "But it *was* addressed to Shadowfield Castle."

"Then who sent it, and where did it come from?"

Erwin told him about the postmaster's note, then reached into his mailbag and gingerly laid the parcel on the table in front of the butler.

Hannes drew back in horror, for the same thought now occurred to him that had been weighing on his listeners' minds ever since he had finished his tale.

"Gentlemen," said the chief, "there is only one way to be sure. Let's open the parcel and be done with it once and for all."

"We can't open it," the postman objected with an almost inaudible whisper. "What about postal regulations?"

"Rubbish," replied the chief. He took the parcel and was about to tear it open when Hannes seized his hand with a strength and determination no one thought he still possessed.

"No, don't touch it," he said quietly. "Let's take it to its rightful owner. Back there, under the old walnut tree."

"You won't catch me going back there alone," said the postman, shaking his head. "No, sir."

"All right," said the chief. "Tomorrow morning the three of us will go. What's there to be afraid of in broad daylight?"

Next morning they all got into the chief's carriage and drove off to Shadowfield. The castle appeared to them as bleak and desolate as ever. Hannes led the way around to the garden and stopped in front of the old walnut tree, crossing himself.

The postman took the parcel out of his mailbag, stepped forward, and quietly laid it on the gnarled, moss-covered roots of the tree. "Delivered," he murmured almost proudly. "May your souls rest in peace," he added, crossing himself.

Behind them the police chief stood quietly, peaked cap in hand. After a while he gently touched his friends' shoulders and told them it was time to go.

The story of Shadowfield Castle and the postman's frightful sighting spread rapidly throughout the mountain town. Some adventurous brats prowled around the dilapidated garden, but the parcel had mysteriously disappeared from under the old walnut tree soon after it was delivered. The castle remains shrouded in darkness and gloom, but no ghost has ever been seen there again.

PART TWO
Haunted Treasures

The Three Partners

ONCE THERE WERE three men: Matthew, a gravedigger; Francis, a poor farmer; and Andrew, a rich shopkeeper. Together they formed a partnership to prospect for gold. Andrew knew of an ancient gold mine that had been deserted for years and put up the money for equipment. For their part, Matthew and Francis chose the proper tools and started working the mine.

The two partners toiled side by side for two days, but on the third day they came to a fork in the main gallery. Here they decided to split up, so Francis took the right tunnel and Matthew the left.

As Francis chipped at the walls along his tunnel, he heard an eerie voice that sounded like a cat's purr: "There is plenty of gold here in exchange for a man's head." At first Francis tried to ignore the voice and just kept working, but then he heard it again: "Give me a man's head, and I'll give you plenty of gold."

Looking up against his will, Francis saw in the dim lamplight a scruffy black tomcat perched on a plank floating in midair. The astonished farmer reached out to pat the creature on its head, but to his even greater amazement, he felt nothing but thin air. I must be very tired, thought Francis, and I'm seeing things. So he took the afternoon off.

For three straight days the strange tomcat appeared to Francis twice a day, always at the same hours: noon and six in the evening. But the brave farmer made up his mind to ignore the mysterious apparition and never mentioned it to his partners. Finally, on the fourth day, the tomcat failed to return, so Francis forgot about it. He went on with his work, but he didn't strike gold.

For his part, Matthew had been working a few days along his tunnel when he heard a chilling caterwaul: "Give me a man's head, and I'll give you plenty of gold." Looking up, he saw a hair-raising sight. There was a scruffy black tomcat strutting on a plank suspended in midair. Instead of a cat's face, however, the creature bore the face of Francis, his partner. The frightful apparition haunted the gravedigger for two days, always at noon and six in the evening. On the third day Matthew could bear it no longer and went to unburden his soul to Andrew.

"The meaning of this vision is plain to see," said the shopkeeper after he had heard Matthew out. "We won't strike gold until we get rid of our partner. For all we know, he's been bargaining with the spirit of the mine* and plotting our deaths."

After talking the matter over, the two crooked partners decided to do Francis in. On the following evening Matthew lay in wait for him at the mouth of the pit. When Francis appeared, Matthew leaped up from behind him and bashed his head in with a shovel. Then he threw the farmer's body into a ravine nearby, leaving him for dead.

With Francis out of the way, Andrew took his place working in the pit, and within a few hours he struck a rich lode of gold. But his greed stifled his joy, and he breathed no word of his find to Matthew. That devilish tomcat really kept its word, thought Andrew. But how do I know that the accursed creature won't make Matthew kill me and rob me of my gold? Better rid myself of him and take his share as well.

Andrew decided he could turn Matthew in to the police for murdering Francis, even though he himself might be charged as an accessory. "But I'd never go to jail," Andrew reasoned, "because now I have plenty of gold to buy off any judge." So the shopkeeper left to file a complaint against his partner and then hurried back to dig for more gold. But Andrew was not fated to enjoy his ill-gotten treasure.

As Matthew worked his tunnel without striking gold, the scruffy tomcat appeared to him again. This time the cat bore the face of Andrew. "Give me a man's head," it meowed, "and I'll give you lots of gold." The tomcat so tormented Matthew that the gravedigger decided to check on his partner. Grabbing his lamp and pick, he headed for the spot where he could hear Andrew chipping away at the rock. Upon entering his partner's tunnel, Matthew saw the thick lode of gold sparkling in the lamplight and was seized by a blind rage. So that's how it is, he thought. That tomcat wasn't lying after all.

As Andrew dug away, oblivious to anything but the sparkle of gold, Matthew sneaked up behind him, raised his pick, and split the shopkeeper's head in two. Stepping callously over his partner's body, the gravedigger held out both his hands toward the precious ore. He had only just touched it when he heard a shuffling noise behind him. Swinging around, Matthew was gripped with terror. In the gloomy lamplight, he saw the pale, gaunt face of Francis, smeared with blood and dirt.

It's the farmer's ghost, thirsting for revenge, thought Matthew, his hair standing on end. He uttered a terrible scream and tried to dash out of the mine, but he tripped over Andrew's corpse and smashed his head against the gold rock.

Francis, puzzled by Matthew's actions, rushed over to see what was wrong. But the gravedigger had stopped breathing. Francis then went over to look at Andrew, who was lying in a heap near the reddish ore, clutching a gold nugget in his frozen hand. He, too, was beyond help, at least in this world.

The poor farmer could make neither head nor tail of what had happened to his partners or, for that matter, to himself. All he could remember was a sharp blow over the head from an unseen hand, and then waking up covered with blood and dirt at the bottom of a ravine. "It's the work of that ghastly tomcat," he had said to himself when he came to. "I must warn Matthew. We should stop prospecting here, because the spirit of the mine is against us." Then Francis had dragged himself out of the ravine and back into the pit, looking for his partner.

As the farmer still pondered what had happened, he suddenly heard the dreaded purr behind him: "The price has been paid. Take all the gold you can carry and leave these parts for good, or you'll end up worse than your partners." This time Francis did not ignore the tomcat's words.

He quickly filled his bags with gold, climbed out of the pit, and took to his heels without glancing back once.

Just as Francis was vanishing around a bend in the road, two constables came up from the village to arrest Matthew for murdering his partner. They descended into the mine and searched it thoroughly. But all they could find were a few rusty old tools, abandoned ages ago. In the end they filed a report stating that the ancient gold mine was deserted and that the three partners had disappeared without a trace.

⊰ The Gypsy Fiddlers ⊱

ONCE THERE WAS an old boyar who was as stingy as he was wealthy. Because he did not want to leave his riches to anyone, he thought up a ghastly scheme. First he sold most of his land and cattle for gold. Then he went to pay a visit to a band of Gypsies who had camped their covered wagons next to his estate.

The old man arrived at the camp in the middle of a merry celebration. The Gypsies were feasting, singing, and dancing to the tunes of five fiddlers, and they invited the boyar to join them. But the old miser turned them down. "I'm here on a pressing errand," he told them. "I'd like you to do me a little favor, and I'll pay you well." Then he asked the Gypsies to follow him with their wagons to the manor house, and they readily agreed.

While the Gypsies waited outside, the boyar had his servants go into the cellar and bring out ten heavy coffers full of gold. "These chests contain magic books," he lied to the Gypsies. "They can work a lot of harm, so I want them out of my house. Load them in your wagons and follow me."

The boyar led the Gypsy caravan to a small cave hidden in a wooded ravine. Under his direction the Gypsies dug a deep hole inside the cave and buried his treasure chests. Then they sealed the mouth of the cave with a brick wall, covering it with dirt and bushes.

After declaring himself satisfied with their labor and swearing them to secrecy, the boyar gave the Gypsies a fat purse of gold. The nomads were surprised by his uncommon generosity. In disbelief they bit into

the gold coins but found them genuine. Since they suspected no other foul play, they thanked the old boyar and drove home.

But that very night the boyar called twenty of his trusted servants and sent them to the Gypsy camp to kill the men who had buried his treasure. Armed to the teeth, the boyar's servants stole up on the sleeping Gypsies and slaughtered them to the last man, woman, and child. They did not spare the five fiddlers either, but ran them through with their swords and smashed their violins into a thousand pieces. After the massacre they took back the boyar's purse of gold, set fire to the covered wagons, and drove the Gypsies' horses into the forest.

Leaving some false traces behind them, the servants rode back to the manor house. The old miser was delighted with the success of the raid and rewarded his men by dividing half of the Gypsies' gold coins among them. Then he had a rumor spread in the village that the Gypsies had been robbed and put to death by highwaymen.

Time went by, the authorities never caught the robbers suspected of having slaughtered the innocent Gypsies, and the heinous deed was forgotten. The boyar grew older and stingier, withdrawing inside his cold, empty mansion. But as his dying hour drew near, he wanted to visit for the last time the spot where his beloved treasure lay buried. Afraid to go there in broad daylight lest someone discover his precious secret, he waited until nightfall and drove out stealthily all by himself.

It was a beautiful summer night with a large full moon, and the boyar could see every tree and bush in the ravine. When he reached the place where his treasure was buried, he got out of his carriage and looked for the cavern. He parted the underbrush and dug through the dirt until he got to the brick wall covering the mouth of the cave. He rested his face against it, sighing contentedly.

Suddenly he heard merry sounds of fiddles and cheerful singing coming from inside. "Someone has stolen my treasure," shrieked the boyar. "You won't get away with it, you filthy robbers. Let me in!" And the old miser started banging frenziedly on the brick wall.

Immediately the wall parted, and he saw the band of Gypsies whom his men had slaughtered years before. They were feasting and dancing to the tunes of their five fiddlers. And the violins that had been broken into a thousand pieces sounded louder and clearer than ever. The boyar screamed with rage and, trying to protect his treasure, hurled himself toward the merrymaking Gypsies. As soon as he crossed the threshold of the brightly lit cavern, the brick wall closed noiselessly behind him.

On a clear summer night passersby can often hear the merry sound of Gypsy fiddles in the wooded ravine where the old boyar had buried his gold, and many have seen a green flame* burning near it. But no one who has dug there has ever found either the cave or the buried treasure, and no one has ever seen or heard of the boyar again.

⇥ The Female Snake ⇤

NOT LONG AGO there lived a poor miner named Gabriel who toiled in a coal mine far away from his village. He spent most of his days in the mine, and his evenings at the alehouse. One night he went to the alehouse for his usual cup of plum brandy and bowl of goulash. Since the place was crowded, Gabriel asked permission to sit at a stranger's table. "Ssertainly," responded the man courteously. "There iss plenty of room here, young man, sso make yoursself at home."

Obviously a foreigner, the stranger seemed very old, yet bore his age with dignity and vigor. He spoke Gabriel's tongue well, except for pronouncing his "s's" with a marked lisp. He was dressed in a spotless white coat, completely out of place in a coal miners' tavern, but Gabriel was drawn to him immediately because of his uncanny eyes, as wise as a serpent's.

The miner struck up a conversation with the old man, and since the foreigner seemed willing to listen, Gabriel started pouring his heart out to him. He spoke of his hard life as a coal miner, and how he had no one to share his troubles with, for he was far away from his village and all alone in the world. The kindly foreigner nodded sympathetically, then ordered several bowls of goulash and another bottle of plum brandy for both of them. Gabriel gratefully ate and drank everything that was set before him.

After the meal the stranger stood up and, placing an ancient gold coin on the table, said with his peculiar, snakelike hiss, "You are a good ssoul, Gabriel. Sso cheer up, becausse from now on you'll never have to be lonely again." Then he left the alehouse with great dignity.

By now the poor miner was so befuddled with the unexpected windfall of brandy, goulash, and gold that he failed to pay much attention to the old man's words. The stranger's coin had covered the entire bill, and Gabriel had enough change left over to order plum brandy and goulash for everyone.

The following morning Gabriel woke up with a splitting headache, having completely forgotten his encounter with the kind foreigner. He dragged himself out of bed as best he could and went to work the early morning shift. That day the miners were clearing land for a new shaft, so many crawling beasts were fleeing the ruthless bulldozers.

Suddenly Gabriel saw a female snake that had stopped in front of his bulldozer and would not budge. He was about to run her over when he noticed her fearless, beautiful eyes, radiating kindness and love. He picked her up and carried her into the woods out of harm's way. But the next morning the snake was back at the clearing waiting for Gabriel. Again she threw him a glance full of love and compassion, such as no maiden had ever given him.

After a while Gabriel grew so fond of the snake that he would never go into the mine without bringing her a bowl of milk and telling her his thoughts. His fellow workers would tease him about his odd conduct, calling the snake his little sweetheart. He laughed good-humoredly along with them, but went right on feeding her and talking to her.

One day when Gabriel and five of his companions were working in the mine, they heard a tremendous blast, and the gallery started shaking as in an earthquake. Terrified, they raced along the pitch-dark tunnels, but everything was collapsing around them. A huge transom fell with a crash, and Gabriel found himself cut off from the rest of the crew. He stopped in his tracks and started calling them at the top of his voice. But from behind the wall of debris there came no answer.

Distraught, Gabriel did not know what to do next, when suddenly he saw his friend, the snake, appear out of nowhere. Leaping and hissing excitedly, she led him to a narrow opening he had not noticed before. He followed her along what seemed an endless crisscross of winding tunnels until finally he caught sight of a ray of light peeping through a crack in the rock above him. A few more minutes of breathless climbing, and he was out in the sunlight, badly shaken but safe.

Gabriel looked around for the snake, but she had disappeared without a trace. His next thought was of his companions trapped down below, so he rushed back to the mine to lend a hand with the rescue operations. But Gabriel never saw his comrades again, for he was the crew's sole survivor.

Stricken with grief, Gabriel decided to give up coal mining and return to his village. He went to say good-bye to the snake, but he could not find her anywhere. Sadly he picked up his bag and stick, leaving that place for good.

Back in his village Gabriel would often think of the beautiful-eyed snake who had saved his life. Then he recalled the old foreigner who had so lavishly treated him to plum brandy and goulash. "That pretty snake," he said to himself with a deep sigh, "must have been a mine spirit whom the old man asked to keep me company."

Since he did not know any other way to make a living, Gabriel went back to mining again. But this time he did not look for work in foreign parts, trying his luck instead with a deserted gold mine outside his village. Without breathing a word to anyone, he borrowed money to buy the digging equipment, loaded everything on his mountain horse, and early one morning climbed to the rocks where the pit stood abandoned.

No sooner had Gabriel gone down the mine shaft than he saw a sight that made his heart leap with joy. There she was, his beautiful-eyed snake, jumping and hissing excitedly. Leading him through a maze of ancient tunnels into a dead end, she curled herself expectantly on top of a huge boulder. There Gabriel started digging, and in no time struck a rich lode of gold. He turned around to thank his companion, but she had again vanished into thin air. How could I not have realized it? thought Gabriel happily. She is obviously a wandering mine spirit, perhaps the old man's daughter. I won't disappoint her. He got down to work and soon filled his saddlebags with as much gold as he could carry. Then he loaded the bags on his horse and went home.

After paying his debts, Gabriel still had enough gold left to buy all the goulash and plum brandy he needed for the rest of his life. A rich man, he never took up mining again. But every summer morning he would ride out of the village with a bottle of fresh milk in his hand and return at noon, whistling happily.

The village folks whispered that Gabriel rode out to meet his little sweetheart, a golden fairy who dwelt in a snake slough. One summer morning a little boy driven by curiosity about the rumor stealthily followed Gabriel all the way to the deserted gold mine. From behind some rocks the boy saw him pour the milk into an empty bowl lying by the mine shaft. Then Gabriel went and sat down in the shade of an oak tree.

Just as the little boy thought he heard some rustling sounds coming out of the pit, he was overpowered by a strange drowsiness and fell sound asleep. When he awoke, the sun was about to set, and the boy looked around him anxiously. Gabriel was nowhere to be seen, but the milk bowl was still there. Trembling with excitement, the boy ran to look at it. The bowl was empty.

⊰ The Six-Fingered Hand ⊱

ONCE THERE WAS a poor man called Elijah who worked as a tollman on the king's highway. Everyone avoided him like the plague, all on account of his left hand, which had six fingers and would never be still.

With those six fingers Elijah could steal whatever he set his eyes on. When he was a little boy, he said, his mother would often kiss the palm of his left hand, causing him to grow a sixth finger. But the village gossip swore that it was not his mother but a spirit in her shape that had kissed his left palm. Be it as it may, this left hand of his was very strong, with fingers long and tough like the teeth of a harrow. If Elijah chose to grab a tree with them, he could uproot it in a flash. Yet he was a peaceful man, unless provoked.

Although a tollman—such men were all reputed to be greedy—Elijah was an honest fellow, living from hand to mouth. He would often get drunk and hum the same little tune, "Loi, loi, loi." His drinking finally cost him his job. But in a way he was glad it did, for now he could spend all day at the gin mill.

With that six-fingered hand of his, Elijah could catch any warbler he chose—nightingale, goldfinch, or skylark. Usually he would lock the birds up in a cage, but when he was in his cups, he would let them go. For Elijah was not a bad sort. He was just marked by the fates, the weird sisters.

He would bring home all kinds of stray beasts and sleep in the same room with dogs, cats, chickens, and geese. His dinner table was always full of mirth and happiness. No matter how starved they were, the dogs would never touch the cats' plates, nor would the cats touch the dogs' bowls. They all lived together in harmony like good brothers and sisters.

These stray beasts were Elijah's only friends, but he was far from lonely. When he was not at the gin mill, he would sit all day long on his porch, surrounded by his animals. And they would gambol and frisk about, while he would sip his plum brandy and tell them about the hard life of a man whom the fates had marked with a six-fingered hand.

Elijah was also famed for a gift of finding gold, but had always kept away from the gold mines and preferred to live in poverty among his beasts. One day, however, he was approached by a gold prospector whom folks had nicknamed Heart-of-Stone. This man was as greedy and pitiless as he was wealthy. Rumor had it that he had hair growing under his tongue, a sign that he was descended from ogres. Other people said he had no human heart in his breast, for no doctor had ever heard it beating. They said, moreover, that in his youth, as he was coming home from the tavern one night, he crossed paths with the spirit of the mine. Since he was in his cups, he grabbed a stone and threw it after her. Then the spirit cursed him: "Let your heart turn to stone." And that was how he got his nickname.

In his greed, Heart-of-Stone thought he could trick Elijah into finding gold for him. He plied him with plum brandy and then hired him to harvest his wheat crop. He took Elijah into the fields next to his gold mine and left him there with his other laborers, asking one of his servants to watch him closely.

At noon the laborers stopped work and went to eat and rest in the shade of a walnut tree. The servant followed them. He pretended to fall asleep, but he watched Elijah like a hawk. After taking a few swigs from his plum brandy bottle, Elijah stretched himself under the tree and started snoring right away. But his six-fingered hand kept working, soon gathering a huge pile of rocks all around the walnut tree. And behold, each rock had big gold nuggets embedded in it.

The servant did not wait for the others to wake up but ran to his master and reported what he had seen. Overjoyed, Heart-of-Stone started back for the field to claim his treasure.

Meanwhile, Elijah awoke and saw all the gold that his magic fingers had raked in. He now realized why Heart-of-Stone had brought him there in the first place, and got very angry at his trickery. He seized the rocks and hurled them with such might that he scattered them all over the hills. By the time Heart-of-Stone arrived, all the gold was gone.

The prospector knew better than to tangle with Elijah, so he had to pay his wages and let him go. Worst of all, from that day forward, Heart-of-Stone's luck turned. His gold mine ran dry, and little by little he lost all his wealth. Then one day his heart of stone cracked inside him. It took six strong men to lift his corpse and lay it in the coffin, so heavily did his heart weigh down on them.

But Elijah, the man with the six-fingered hand, went on living his carefree life among his yard beasts, drinking his plum brandy and humming his little tune, "Loi, loi, loi."

The Red Rose

O<small>NCE THERE WERE</small> two families, one rich, the other poor. The rich family had an only son, Alexander, who was honest and hardworking. The poor one had an only daughter, Elena, who was the most beautiful and sensible maiden in the village. The two youngsters grew up together and had loved each other ever since they could remember.

Even though Alexander's parents liked Elena, they wanted a daughter-in-law with a large dowry and threatened to disinherit their son if he married without their blessing. As the youth loved Elena dearly, he went digging for gold in an abandoned mine, to provide his bride with the dowry his parents demanded. Yet, although he dug for a whole year, he found not so much as an ounce of gold.

In that village, during the long winter evenings, young maidens would gather and sit together at an old woman's cottage. They would spin or card wool, tell stories, and gossip about the latest goings-on in the village. Sometimes the young lads would also drop by to keep the maidens company, courting them in jest or in earnest. Many a splendid village wedding had its humble beginnings in these gatherings.

On such evenings Alexander would often come by the old woman's house to visit with Elena, and the maiden eagerly awaited his arrival. The young couple would laugh and talk together until it was time for Elena to go home. Then Alexander would always accompany her through the huge snowbanks as far as her gate. Nothing unseemly had ever passed between them, because Alexander was an honorable young man and Elena a wise and honest girl.

Once Alexander had a cup of plum brandy too many and, while

accompanying Elena home, tried to steal a kiss from her. She became flustered and rebuked him gently, begging him to wait until they were engaged. Thereupon Alexander, who had a rash temper, grew angry and swore that he would not wed her until a red rose blossomed in the bowels of the earth. To make matters worse, he even called upon the spirit of the mine to be his witness. Appalled at such foolishness, the maiden started crying and parted from him heartbroken. Yet all night she prayed that no harm would come to him in the mine.

The following morning Alexander woke up feeling sorry about his ill-considered oath, but now it was too late. Besides, he was too ashamed to go and ask Elena for forgiveness. Ruefully he picked up his tools and started for the pit.

As the youth was about to descend into the mine shaft, he was startled to find an old man standing next to him. The stranger had a long, white beard and was dressed in plain peasant clothes. "Good day, my boy," said the stranger.

"Good day to you, too, old man," replied Alexander. "But what brings you to our valley, for I've never seen you around here before."

"Well, my boy, I used to dig for gold in these parts long before you or your parents were born."

"Alas, old man, you shouldn't have troubled to come back. I've been digging here for a whole year without finding one grain of gold."

"Maybe so, but I remember a tiny gallery that looked promising. I didn't work it properly last time around, for I had to leave in a hurry. Why don't you and I become partners? Should we strike gold, we'll take equal shares."

The lad readily agreed. Thereupon the old man guided him through a maze of dark and musty passages covered with cobwebs and swarming with rats and crawling beasts. This was a part of the mine the youth had never seen before. He had a hard time keeping up with the old man, who seemed to be able to find his way even without the light from his companion's carbide lamp. Alexander grew more and more uneasy. Suddenly a gang of squealing bats swooped down on them, and he began to regret having entered into a rash partnership with a man he didn't know.

"It won't be long now," said the old man, as though guessing the youth's gloomy thoughts.

The tunnel grew lower and lower, until Alexander had to crawl on all fours. But soon they came to a high-vaulted cave shrouded in darkness. "This is the spot, if I'm not mistaken," said the old man. "Now it's up to you, my boy." And he sat down on a boulder, lighting his pipe.

The lad was tired and had a strange feeling about the mysterious cavern. At first he could not see much and could hear only the flutter of bat wings mingled with the faint murmur of water trickling down the cavern walls. But when he held up his lamp and examined the rock, he thought he was dreaming. In the faint light the rock was glistening not only with dewy moisture but also with the finest red gold.

Alexander's heart leaped with joy, and he entirely forgot his fatigue. Taking out his tools, he fell to chipping away at the rock. In a few hours he had filled his two bags with large nuggets of gold. He gave one of the bags to the old man.

The stranger looked at his share gleefully. "We didn't do too badly for half a day's work, did we, my boy?" he said. "Now all your troubles are over, for your worthy bride will get a dowry fit for a queen. I'll tell you what. Set a date for your wedding right away, and I'll give her my share of gold as a wedding present."

"Alas, old man," answered the youth, suddenly becoming rueful again and not daring to ask the stranger whence he knew so much about his affairs. "How can I wed her when I swore a solemn oath that I'd never take her for my wife unless a red rose blossomed in the bowels of the earth?"

"That was a foolish oath indeed," said the old man with a laugh, "but this once we'll let it pass. You were in your cups and didn't know what you were saying. Turn your lamp toward the far end of the cavern."

Alexander held out his lamp toward the depths of the cave, and what he saw sent a shiver through him. He turned the light back toward the old man, but he had disappeared. Alarmed, he quickly glanced at the cave wall again. His eyes had played no tricks on him, for burning in the rock with a bright red flame was a magnificent lode of gold in the shape of a rose in full bloom.

With tears of gratitude rolling down his cheeks, Alexander thanked the invisible old man. "Don't thank me," he heard a voice out of nowhere say. "Thank your wise and pure betrothed, who prayed for you last night. Hurry back home and ask her to forgive you."

Alexander did not wait to be told twice. Grabbing his bags of gold, he rushed back to the village. Once there, he showed Elena the gold and humbly asked her for forgiveness, which she readily granted. And before the month was out, they celebrated their wedding in the very cavern where the wondrous rose of their true love had blossomed.

The Ancient Fortress

MANY YEARS AGO, when Transylvania was still plagued by unjust rulers, there lived an upright old miller named Benjamin. Because of his honesty, people came from all over with grain for Benjamin to mill. Consequently the old miller had become very rich. Many folk also thought him a wizard, believing that he could conjure up gold from the depths of the earth, and with the help of wolfsbane, a magic weed, open any iron lock without a key.

Because God had granted Benjamin not only wealth but also a long life, he had outlived his wife and even his sons, so now he was left all by himself. He had one close friend—Constantin, a poor but honest old farmer with two hardworking sons. Benjamin spent the better part of each day with Constantin, often observing that there was no greater treasure on earth than friendship.

One Sunday the two old friends sat talking on the porch of the mill. "Brother Constantin, we have been friends a long time," said Benjamin. "And so I'd like to help you and your sons lead the kind of life you deserve. You know I have the reputation of being a wizard. This may or may not be true, but I want to share a secret with you. Many years ago I gave food and shelter to a dying old hermit. On his deathbed he gave me a magic box containing wolfsbane and a yellow candle. He told me that the magic weed could open any iron gate in the world, and that the burning candle could reveal any buried treasure, while changing its guardians to stone. But all of this can be done only on Midsummer's Eve before the stroke of midnight."

"Is this magic box the reason for your wealth, my friend?" asked Constantin.

"Not at all," answered Benjamin. "I've never tested its powers, because I've earned everything I own by honest work. But now I'm of a mind to lend this magic box to you and your sons."

"If this is your wish," said Constantin, "let's test it together, for it was your charity that the old hermit wanted to reward. You know that ancient, ruined fortress near our village. Some folks believe that beneath it there lies a fabulous treasure, but that no one can get to it because of the spirits who guard it. Let's go there on Midsummer's Eve to test the powers of your magic box."

On the appointed day Benjamin and Constantin, with his two sons, set out on horseback for the ancient ruins, perched on the top of a thickly wooded hill a few miles away from their village. When they reached the hilltop, it was after sunset, and they could barely see the dilapidated walls and towers overgrown with weeds and brambles. Constantin lit an oil lamp, and they started looking for the iron gate, which lay half-buried in the ground. Once they found it, Benjamin touched it with the wolfsbane from the magic box. At once they heard a tremendous crash, and Constantin's lamp went out with a sputter.

Plunged into darkness, they could hear strange, harsh voices and the clanking of weapons growing louder and louder. Benjamin did not lose heart, but lit the hermit's candle, and the frightening noises ceased. A pleasant fragrance of myrrh enveloped them, and they found themselves in a beautiful garden in full bloom, with strange, colorful birds in the trees and swarms of bees on pink and white blossoms. Strangest of all, all the creatures stood still, suspended in midair.

In the middle of the enchanted garden Benjamin and his friends saw a dazzling crystal palace that seemed deserted. Inside the palace they came to the top of a white marble staircase that led down into a spacious hall lit by a hundred torches. An ominous silence surrounded them, and they became so frightened that they could not decide whether to walk on down the stairs or turn back. But in the end the thought of fabulous riches drove them forward.

Upon entering the huge hall, they were dazed by a wondrous sight. Everywhere there were mounds of glittering gold watched by fierce dogs, and in the middle there was a large silver coffer full of rubies and diamonds blazing in the bright torchlight. The magnificent coffer was guarded by two angry lions. Surrounding the lions were tall, bearded soldiers with halberds and swords pointed toward the intruders.

The adventurers were about to withdraw in terror when they noticed that the dogs, the lions, and the soldiers were as still as the birds and the bees in the enchanted garden. Even the tails of the angry lions were frozen in mid-twitch. The guardians of the treasure could roll their eyes and clearly were aware of the strangers, but they could not harm them. The light of Benjamin's magic candle had frozen them in their tracks.

Constantin and his sons took heart and stepped up to the mounds of gold and gems, filling their saddlebags to the brim. Even Benjamin, who had enough wealth as it was, could not resist stuffing his coat pockets with a few precious stones. Well before midnight he motioned to the others that they should depart, and led the party up the marble staircase, out of the palace, and into the garden.

As soon as they arrived at the iron gate and Benjamin blew out the magic candle, they heard the cock crow. Immediately they heard another tremendous crash, and the enchanted garden disappeared. The lights went out, leaving them stranded amid the dark, eerie ruins.

At that instant the full moon rose above the hillcrest, and they saw their horses waiting patiently for them at the edge of the forest. They climbed into the saddle and reached home before daybreak without any trouble. Overjoyed, Constantin and his sons commended Benjamin for his generosity and courage, and then went to bury their treasure in a safe place.

Not long thereafter the old miller and his friends were seized and brought before the throne of the ruler. The ruler's spies had reported to him that Benjamin had employed wizardry in order to turn Constantin and his sons into wealthy men. A greedy, coldhearted man, the ruler intended to sentence the innocent men to death and confiscate their estates.

"You stand accused of using murder and witchcraft to make yourselves rich. What do you have to say in your defense?"

"Your Highness," began Benjamin, speaking for all of them. "We didn't harm anyone. As for witchcraft, we had no communion with evil spirits but only with the powers of light." Then he told the ruler about the magic box and the enchanted palace hidden beneath the ancient ruins.

At the mention of mounds of gold and gems, the ruler's eyes sparkled with greed. He promised to release the prisoners if Benjamin would lead him to the treasure, and the old miller agreed to do just that. The very next Midsummer's Eve he took the ruler and ten of his most trusted servants to the wooded hilltop on which stood the ruined fortress. He warned them not to be scared of anything they would see, to take only the riches they could carry, and, most important, to leave the treasure hall before midnight.

But the ruler was too impatient to listen to Benjamin's advice, ordering him to open the rusty iron gate without any further delay. So Benjamin touched it with the wolfsbane, whereupon the gate flew open with a thundering crash. Then he lit the magic candle, and behold, the ancient ruins vanished. In their place appeared again the beautiful garden in bloom and the dazzling crystal palace. Once inside, they walked down the white marble staircase and entered the torchlit hall full of priceless treasures. At the sight of the fierce dogs, lions, and armed guards, the ruler was gripped with fear. However, once he noticed that these dangers were as lifeless as the enchanted garden, he rushed to the mounds of riches and ordered his men to take everything with them. They filled their sacks with gold and then turned to the huge silver coffer, but the ten strong servants could barely lift it, let alone carry it.

As midnight approached, Benjamin began to urge them to leave, but the greedy ruler and his men ignored him, trying to find a means of carrying all the treasures at once. Seeing that there was no reasoning with them, Benjamin walked silently up the stairs and into the garden. Then he blew out the magic candle. Instantly there came another tremendous crash, the enchanted garden and palace vanished, and Benjamin found himself all alone amid the dark ruins. The evil ruler and his men had been swallowed up by the earth.

Satisfied, the old miller mounted his horse and returned to his friends. After telling them about the dreadful fate of the tyrant, he threw the magic box into the river, for they had more than enough riches.

As for the greedy ruler and his men—today anyone passing those ancient ruins on a clear Midsummer's Eve can still hear their sobs and wails rising from the depths of the earth and can see a green flame dancing on the iron gate.

PART THREE
Eerie Fairy Tales

⊰ The Dark Stranger ⊱

ONCE UPON A TIME there was an ancient mill built of sturdy logs. The miller was an honest soul, if somewhat rash, with three hardworking sons. He had inherited the mill from his father, who had it from his father, who had it from his father. The great-grandfather had bought it from a stranger, who had then disappeared without a trace.

One fine evening a blind old beggar walked into the mill yard and asked for a crust of bread. The kindhearted miller called on his wife to treat the old man to the best supper she could put together.

"Come in," said the miller's wife, leading the blind man across the threshold into the kitchen. She seated him at the table and gave him a steaming bowl of lamb stew with a thick slice of fresh peasant bread. Then she asked her eldest son to go down to the cellar and draw a jug of wine for the old man.

"Let him draw it himself," the boy replied, leaving the room in a huff. Ashamed, the woman apologized to the blind man and turned to her middle son.

"Is spring water not good enough for him?" asked the middle son, and he, too, left, slamming the kitchen door. Thereupon the miller's youngest son went down to the cellar and drew a jug of wine for their guest, bringing back not the cheap kind but the finest wine they had.

The old man ate and drank in silence. Having finished, he thanked his hosts and stood up to leave.

"Stay as long as you wish," said the miller's wife. "There is plenty of room behind the brick stove, where you'll be warm and snug."

The old man accepted her invitation gratefully and sat down by the large kitchen stove. After a while the miller came in for his supper. Just as he finished and was about to go to bed, there were three knocks on the kitchen door. Opening it, the miller saw a tall, swarthy stranger in an old-fashioned black velvet costume and a black-plumed hat. He was riding a fiery black stallion.

Without dismounting, the dark stranger threw three sacks of grain down by the door and said, "Grind this wheat for me, my good Christian. But you must grind it very fine and only after dark. I'll be back two evenings hence, and if you have it ready for me, you'll get another purse just like this one." With these words the stranger leaned over and thrust a silk purse into the hand of the bedazzled miller. Then he rode off without further ado.

When the miller opened the purse, he found three sparkling gold pieces, the likes of which he had never seen before. Overjoyed, he showed them to his wife and said he would start the job right away.

"That would be mighty foolish," put in the blind old beggar from his corner.

"What would you know about it, old man?" The miller turned to him impatiently. "You couldn't even see the fine gentleman and his gold."

"True, I'm blind, but I see what I see," replied the old man. "Don't touch that grain, or you'll come to grief."

The miller told him to mind his own business and go to sleep. Then he carried the sacks into the mill and made ready to grind the stranger's wheat. As soon as he opened the first sack, his heart sank, for the grain looked like pitch-black iron pellets. But then he thought of the gold pieces and poured the grain into the chute.

When he checked the huge millstones, the miller saw they were not grinding the wheat, so he readjusted them, but to no avail. Every time he poured the black kernels in, they came out without even a scratch on them. "What sort of wheat is this?" he asked himself, and dipped his hand into the sack. But as he touched the grain, a strange drowsiness came over him, and he had to go and lie down. Since no one was about except his eldest son, the miller asked him to grind the stranger's wheat and immediately fell into a deep slumber.

At daybreak the miller went to see whether his son had had better luck than he with the black wheat. And behold, the first sack was filled to the brim with finely ground flour, white as snow. He looked for his son but could not find him, so he reckoned the lad had gone to town and thought no more of it.

The miller tended to his usual business, but in the evening he followed the stranger's instructions and opened the second sack. Inside it he found the same pitch-black wheat, and no sooner had he touched it than he was again overcome by drowsiness. He went to lie down, and since everyone was asleep except his middle son, he asked him to grind the stranger's wheat.

Around midnight the miller's youngest son was awakened by a great rumble. The mill was grinding so fast that the whole house shook, and above the infernal din he thought he heard his middle brother's voice. Try as he would, the boy could not awaken his parents. Hurrying outside, he heard his brother crying, "Help, help me, Father! Was I not your obedient son?"

The boy rushed to the doors of the shaking mill only to find them locked. He peeped inside through a small crack, and shrank back in horror. Amid a whirling cloud of dust and light, the stranger was spinning the mighty millstone at a dizzying speed, as if it were a well-greased wheel of fortune. The frightened boy caught just a glimpse of his brother's horridly twisted face as it went under the grindstone.

Suddenly the cock crowed for midnight, and the mill became still as a grave, its doors slowly swinging open in the moonlight. The boy screwed up his courage and stepped inside. The stranger and his stallion had vanished, but so had his brother. The grindstones bore no mark of their gory work, and all that the boy could see was an open sack filled to the brim with finely ground, snow-white flour.

As the boy rushed toward the house to awaken his parents, out came the blind beggar. "No use waking them up," said the old man, "for there's nothing they or you can do tonight."

"What is this all about?" asked the boy wildly.

"Now, listen to me carefully. That stranger is here to collect on an

ancient debt. A hundred fifty years ago, he sold the mill to your great-great-grandfather. Since your ancestor could not pay for it in full, the stranger challenged him to a game of dice. Should your great-great-grandfather win, he would get the mill for free. Should he lose, the stranger would get his great-great-grandchildren's souls. The stranger won the bet, so now he has come for payment. But the other night you proved to me that you are a kindhearted boy, so I'll tell you how to rid yourself of the debt.

"Tomorrow at daybreak," the blind man continued, "go to the monastery up the hill and ask the monks for holy water. Then take three handfuls of the stranger's flour, knead it with holy water, and ask your mother to bake a small loaf of bread. Breathe no word of this to your father and wait till he asks you to help him with the black wheat. Then go to the mill, but whatever you do, don't touch the grain, for it will take away your strength. Once the stranger arrives, remain silent and show him the loaf of bread. If you stand your ground till the cock crows, you will never hear from him again."

The old man tapped his way back into the kitchen and climbed behind the brick stove, where he had remained unnoticed since the evening before. But the miller's son tarried in the yard, for he could not sleep from grief over his brothers. And as soon as he heard the monastery bell tolling for matins, he went and did everything the old man had told him to do.

At nightfall the miller came back from the mill as tired as ever and asked his youngest son to grind the stranger's last sack of wheat. "He's due to pick up his flour tonight," said the miller, so overcome by drowsiness that you could have knocked him over with a feather.

Once his parents fell asleep, the lad walked over to the mill, hiding under his shirt the loaf of bread his mother had baked for him. Just before midnight he heard hoofbeats outside. Suddenly the mill doors flew open, and in rode the dark stranger on his fiery stallion.

"I see, my dear boy, you didn't get the job done." He chuckled, and with his little finger he started spinning the huge millstone as if it were a weathercock. "You're no better than your brothers and will join them soon enough."

In a flash he drove his horse toward the miller's son, ready to grab him. But the lad kept a steady heart and did not budge an inch. He took the holy bread out of his shirt and held it out to the stranger. At the sight of the loaf, the stallion reared wildly and threw his rider under the grindstone. At that very instant the cock crowed for midnight, and with a tremendous neigh the stallion leaped into the mill after his master. Then all was quiet, and the lad saw that the third sack had filled up with soot.

The miller's son ran into the kitchen to thank the old man for his help. "Could you please save my brothers, too?" he pleaded. "They are a bit rash, like my father, but they mean well."

"So be it," said the blind beggar. "But let this be a lesson to them." Then he told the lad how he could bring them back to life.

Hearing the matins bell, the miller's son fetched holy water from the monks again. He mixed the sack of soot in with the two sacks of snow-white flour.* Then he added the holy water, made two loaves in the shape of his brothers, and put them into the brick oven, all as instructed by the old man. Soon he looked into the oven, and lo and behold, there were his brothers, just waking up.

When the older brothers learned how the blind beggar had saved their lives, they felt ashamed. They looked for him behind the brick stove to ask his forgiveness, but the old man had melted into thin air.

Full of wonder, the three brothers went to awaken their parents and gave them a full account of what had occurred during the past three nights. The miller was overjoyed at having his sons back safe and sound, and he threw a magnificent feast to which he invited the whole village and seven bands of Gypsy fiddlers. And they would be feasting still, had they not run out of meat and wine.

⇌ The Red Emperor's Son ⇌

ONCE THERE WAS a red emperor who bought himself food for ten ducats. After eating some of it, he put the rest in his larder under lock and key. But overnight someone broke into the larder and stole all his food. The emperor was furious and proclaimed that he would give half his kingdom to whoever caught the thief. So the red emperor's oldest son went to his father and said, "May God grant you a long life, Father dear, but why give half your kingdom to a stranger? I'll try to catch the thief myself."

"So be it," replied the emperor, "but have you no fear of what you might encounter?"

"I fear nothing," bragged the oldest son, and that night he went to keep watch over his father's larder. He lay awake for a while, but just before midnight a warm wind started blowing and soon lulled him to sleep. When he awoke at daybreak, the youth saw that the larder had again been tampered with. He was so ashamed that he left his father's house for good.

The next day the middle son went before his father and asked to be allowed to stand watch.

"Do as you wish, my son," said the emperor, "but take care not to lose face the way your elder brother did."

"Never fear, Father," said the middle son with a laugh, and that very evening he went to bed in the chamber next to the larder. But as soon as he laid his head on the pillow, a warm wind started blowing, and he was overcome by sleep. The following morning the larder was empty, and the middle son also left his father's house in disgrace.

Now Peter, the youngest son, tried to prove his worth. Before he lay down by the larder, he stuck four needles in his pillow so that every time his head nodded, one of the needles would prick him and keep him awake. And so it went till a little before midnight. Then he saw a horrifying sight that made his hair stand on end. His little sister rose from her cradle, turned three somersaults, and changed into a hideous creature with nails like scythes and teeth like scimitars. She flew to the larder, broke it open with her sharp claws, and wolfed down all the food she found there. Then she lay back in her cradle and wrapped herself in her swaddles, becoming a sweet baby girl again.

The youth thought he would never live to see another sunrise. At daybreak he went straight to his father, who, noticing his wild look, asked him, "What did you see, Peter?"

"Alas, Father," replied the youth, "it would have been better if I had dozed off like my brothers and had seen nothing. Please give me a horse and a chest full of gold, for I wish to go into the wide world in search of a bride."

His father said nothing but immediately granted his son's request. The youngster rode out of the castle and dug a hole in the ground not too far from the emperor's well. There he buried his treasure chest, marking the place with a pile of stones.

For a long time he wandered till he came to the woodpecker, the queen of the birds.

"Where are you going, Peter?" asked the queen.

"Where there is neither death nor old age, to find myself a bride."

"You've come to the right place," said the queen.

"How is that?"

"Do you see those woods that stretch forever? Only when I've pecked through every tree will old age and death come to me."

"One peck today, another tomorrow," said Peter, "and sooner or later old age and death will catch up with you. No, this isn't the place for me." Bidding the woodpecker farewell, he rode on.

After a long journey Peter came to a copper palace. Out of it ran a beautiful young maiden who kissed and embraced him. The lad spent several days at the palace, where he was treated like a king. When he said he wanted to leave, and why, the maiden begged him to stay. "See the high mountains over there?" she asked Peter. "Old age and death will come to these parts only when the mighty wind cuts those mountains down to molehills. Why don't you remain here with me?"

"Thank you," replied the youth, "but I must ride on to look for the abode of the mighty wind."

The youth wandered on till he reached the end of this world, whereupon his horse said to him, "Master dear, give me four whiplashes and yourself two, so that we can cross the Vale of Longing. Should Longing try to wrestle you out of the saddle, spur me on as hard as you can and never as much as look back."

Peter did as his horse told him, and after crossing the Vale of Longing safely, they arrived at a tiny hut in the other world. There he saw a handsome boy who looked about fifteen years younger than Peter.

"What brought you here, Peter?" asked the boy.

"I've come in search of a place where there's neither old age nor death."

"You've come to the right spot," said the boy, "for I am the wind."

"In that case I'll stay with you forever," declared Peter. And there he remained for thousands and thousands of years without growing any older.

Then one day Peter went hunting among the nearby hills of gold and silver, but brought home no game. The wind warned him, "Peter, you can roam all over those hills, but take care not to cross back into the Vale of Longing, or you'll be done for."

Peter promised to be careful, but a few hundred years later, while chasing a golden deer, he followed her unawares into the Vale of Longing. And this time Longing caught up with him and wrestled him to the ground. As Peter returned to the wind's hut, his eyes were swimming in tears. "I can't stay here any longer," he said. "I wish to go back to my father."

"What foolishness is this?" replied the wind. "Your father's long gone, and so are your brothers. No one can even remember the place where your town once stood. In fact, I passed by that very spot less than an hour ago. They were sowing wheat all over it."

But Peter was sick with longing, so he ignored the wind's words. He bade him farewell, mounted his horse, and soon arrived at the young maiden's copper palace. The high mountains near it had already turned into molehills, and no one ran out to welcome him. When a crone finally answered his knock at the palace gate, Peter could barely recognize her as the beautiful young maiden he had once known. No sooner had she set eyes on him than she gave a feeble cry, instantly turning to dust. Peter mourned her for several days, but then moved on.

Next he came to the home of the woodpecker queen. Only one tree was left of the endless woods around her castle, and the queen was all shriveled up and wrinkled with age. Upon seeing him, she exclaimed, "Peter, how can you still look so young?"

Then the woodpecker queen pecked through the last branch of her tree, and fell to the ground lifeless. Peter buried her, and then went on his way.

When he finally came to the place where the red emperor's town had once stood, Peter found nothing there but a field of wheat. Recognizing his father's ancient well, the youth rode up to it, searching for the stone mound beneath which he had buried his treasure chest. He saw a pile of rocks behind some elder bushes, and an old man sitting on it with a white beard reaching down to his waist.

"Old man," said Peter, "can you tell me what happened to the red emperor's town that stood here not long ago? I am the red emperor's son."

"Is that so?" replied the old man. "I think the father of my father once mentioned a red emperor. But there's been no town here ever since I can remember."

"Yet it seems only yesterday that I left my father's castle. Here, old man, move over and I'll prove it to you."

Peter drew his sword and started digging under the stone mound where he had buried his gold. He dug for three days until he reached the treasure chest. But when he opened it, he recoiled in horror. Inside on a pile of gold lay his baby sister.

"Aha, you've finally come back to me," she croaked. Instantly she jumped out of the box, turning into a hideous crone with nails like scythes and teeth like scimitars.

"Get him, Death," said the old man.

"No, you get him first, Old Age," said the crone.

As soon as Old Age wrestled Peter to the ground, Death dug her claws into him and ate him up. Then they took his treasure and horse, and threw them to the wind.

⚊ The Wheel of Fire ⚊

ONCE UPON A TIME there was an old couple who had twins, a boy and a girl. The parents were very poor, but they loved the twins dearly and often went hungry themselves in order to have enough to feed their children. Yet the twins were too young to understand the plight of their parents, so one day the boy complained to his twin, "If we remain in this house much longer, sister dear, we'll starve to death. Let's go into the wide world in search of better parents."

His sister agreed, and the twins set out at daybreak. The evening found them in the middle of a large plain. Tired and hungry, they sought shelter, but all they could see were desolate flatlands stretching for miles on end. Suddenly a huge black dog came upon them, snarling viciously. The frightened twins ran from it across the plain as fast as they could. After what seemed an endless chase, the children spotted a light in the distance and soon came to a manor house.

When the twins reached the main gate, the ferocious beast stopped chasing them. Jumping over the tall fence, it disappeared into the garden behind the house. The children knocked on the gate, but there was no answer. They tried the handle and found the gate unlocked. They crossed the yard quickly for fear of the dog and walked into the house. Inside the kitchen they saw a table laden with all kinds of dainty dishes, so they ate their fill. Then, cold and tired, they lay down behind the warm brick stove and soon fell asleep.

Around midnight the twins were awakened by loud barking and cursing. Suddenly the kitchen door flew open, and a man rushed in followed by the same black dog that had chased them earlier in the evening. Man and beast started rolling on the floor, locked in a deadly fight. The man finally managed to grab the dog by the scruff of its neck and reached out for a large kitchen knife. But before the man could slit its throat, the dog shook itself free and leaped through the open window, vanishing into the night.

"Next time you won't be so lucky," the man shouted after the beast, and then came up to the brick stove. The moonlight revealed his face. He was a ghastly old creature with small, viper-like eyes and dark, shriveled skin. Glaring at the children, he snapped, "What are you hiding there for? I saw you come in to my kitchen and gorge yourselves on my food. From now on, you must earn your keep. There are enough chores around this house to last you forever. And don't even dream of running away, for you know who's waiting for you outside."

With these nasty words the old man left, and everything became silent again. The children were frightened, but there was nothing they could do except comfort each other, and soon they fell back to sleep.

The next morning the twins saw an old woman moving about in the kitchen. She was very pale, with thin yellow hands. She smiled kindly at the children, telling them her name was Kate. She gave them some work to do in the kitchen and showed them what to eat for supper.

"No matter what you hear or see tonight," Kate whispered to the twins, "don't come out from behind the stove." With that warning she walked out and was gone for the day. Whenever the children came close to the door or the window, they heard the dog growling outside. It would also scratch frenziedly at the kitchen door, trying to break in and get them.

In the evening, once the twins settled behind the brick stove, they again heard loud barking and cursing around the house. The door burst open, and in tumbled the old man with the vicious black beast on top of him. Both were covered with blood, and the old man reached for the kitchen knife. But again the dog managed to escape through the window. The man swore at it angrily and left the room without paying any attention to the terrified children.

The following morning Kate came back into the kitchen, whispering to the twins, "Watch out tonight, for this may be your chance." The children worked hard all day. At dusk they lighted an oil lamp and went to lie down behind the stove, bracing themselves for the night's renewed horrors.

And sure enough, toward midnight the dreadful barking and cursing started all over again, and now it was so loud that it shook the whole house. Soon the old man and the black beast broke through the kitchen door, wrestling fiercely. The old man seized the knife again, but this time the dog went straight for his throat. The man managed to foil the attack by pushing his fist into the beast's gaping mouth and grabbing its tongue. In the next instant he slit the dog's throat.

Blood splattered the kitchen walls, and the children heard a ghastly death rattle that became more and more human. They peeped from behind the stove, and to their horror, the dog's shaggy body had changed into a man's before their very eyes. But what frightened them most was that the corpse looked just like the old man himself.

Screaming, the twins jumped out from behind the stove and ran out of the house. Behind them they heard all kinds of chasing noises, scurrying of feet, galloping of horses, cursing, and catcalling. But they never looked back and kept running until they reached a farmhouse.

The farmer was checking on his animals when he saw the two scared children rushing toward him. He took his ax and stepped into the middle of the road. Just as the children hid behind the barn, a wheel of fire came rolling down the road, heading straight for the farmer. The man jumped aside and took a swing at it with his ax, but missed. The burning wheel rolled on and leaped into the farmer's well with a sinister hiss.

"Quickly," said the farmer, who did not seem surprised by the wheel's odd behavior. "Let's get it out of there, or it will dry up my well." He fished the now smoking wheel out of the well and nailed it up on the side of the barn. "Don't be scared, children," he said. "Just look at it."

The wheel quickly lost its round shape and turned into a shriveled old man, hanging on the barn wall. "There is nothing we can do to keep this restless soul from coming and going as he pleases," the farmer said. "By morning he'll be gone again." He invited the children inside and, after offering them a glass of fresh milk, told them the story of the old man.

Long ago the evil ghost had been a wizard who had a twin brother and a younger sister. He poisoned them in order to take over their inheritance, but instead of letting them rest in their graves, he kept them in his power as servants. By sprinkling his brother with the fresh and innocent blood of twins, he changed him into a huge black dog to guard his estate. Their poor sister he had forced to become the cook.

Eventually the old wizard died, but he still held sway over his siblings. Every night the twins got into a fierce fight, and occasionally the old man would cut the dog's throat. When that happened, the beast would become human again and could return to his grave to rest at last in peace, unless the wizard again sprinkled it with the blood of twins. The old man forced the poor dog itself to go out and find new victims, so that he would never run out of the fresh blood he needed for his grisly witchcraft.

"Passersby," added the farmer, "often report that late at night they've sighted a brightly lit house in the middle of the plain. Yet all one can see there in the daytime is endless fields of wheat. I for one have never

set eyes on this house, but the old man turns up in my yard now and then, as he did today. Don't worry, though, for he seems powerless outside his home."

For their part, the twins told the farmer about the terrifying goings-on at the wizard's estate, and he was glad to have his story confirmed. In the morning they all went to look at the old man hanging from the barn wall. But the wizard was gone.

The twins thanked the farmer for saving their lives and hurried back home. They now understood how good and loving their old parents were, and never again complained about being hungry.

⊰ The Wicked Queen ⊱

ONCE UPON A TIME there was an old king, and his young queen bore him a baby boy who grew faster in one day than others in a month. But soon after the birth of his son, the king died while hunting in the forest. The boy became bored in his mother's castle, so he left home in search of adventures.

The boy rode on and on until he reached a huge forest, in the middle of which stood a castle inhabited by twelve monsters. He knocked on the castle gate, but no one answered. Entering anyway, he saw a dirk hanging from a nail. He took the weapon and hid behind the gate, waiting for the monsters' return. Luckily the creatures did not all arrive at the same time, so the boy cut off their heads one by one, piling them up in the cellar. But the youngest monster was too quick for him and wrestled the dirk out of his hand. After a fierce fight, the boy overpowered him as well and sealed him up inside a barrel. Then he took over the monsters' castle.

One day the boy went for a walk in the forest and came upon another castle. In that castle lived a little girl who was even braver and smarter than he was. They instantly took a liking to each other. The boy told her that he had slain eleven monsters, but had left one alive, sealing him inside a barrel. "It's a pity you didn't kill him," said the girl, "for he'll give you many a headache."

The boy invited her to move in with him and his mother, the queen, whom he wanted to bring to the forest castle.

"Bring her," said the little girl, "but you'll regret it." And although she agreed to be his bride, she would not go live with them.

The boy went to fetch his mother and showed her around the monsters' castle. "You can walk freely through all these chambers," he said to her, "but keep out of the cellar, which should always stay locked."

"Never fear, my son," promised his mother. "I won't even dream of going down there."

But one day, while the boy was hunting in the forest, his mother unlocked the cellar, lighted a candle, and went in. Lying around was a pile of frightful skulls and bones, and next to them stood a huge barrel. The queen's curiosity was stronger than her fear. She unsealed the barrel, and out came an ugly monster who said, "My gracious Queen, bring me a little water, and I'll be your obedient servant."

After she granted his request, the monster cooed, "I love you so, my beautiful Queen. Will you marry me?"

"I will," replied the queen.

"But first we must get rid of your dreadful son," said the monster. "Pretend that you're ill and will get better only if he brings you a piglet from the sow who dwells at the earth's edge."

She took to her bed at once. When her son came home and saw her lying in bed, he asked, "What's wrong with you, Mother?"

"I am very ill, my dear son," lied the queen. "I dreamed that I would soon die unless I ate a piglet from the sow who dwells at the earth's edge."

At the thought of his mother's death the poor boy began to weep, and he went to ask his bride for advice.

"Go, if you must," said the girl. "But be careful lest the sow catch you, because she'll swallow you whole. Take my six-winged horse, and be sure to stop here on your way home."

The youth mounted the magic horse, and in a flash they arrived at the earth's edge. The sow was enjoying her afternoon nap, so the lad sneaked up to her; he grabbed one of her piglets, and off he went. Hearing the piglet's loud squeals, the sow woke up and started chasing after them. Just as the magic horse was about to fly back over the earth's edge, the sow grabbed his tail and snapped it off. But she could no longer harm them, for they had crossed over to the other side.

The lad then stopped to see his bride before going home. Without his knowledge she took his piglet and replaced it with another. The deceitful queen cooked and ate the girl's piglet, saying that it had done her a world of good. But three or four days later she pretended to be taken sick again, at the monster's request.

"I had another dream, my son," lied the queen. "I must have a golden apple from the other realm or I shall perish."

The distraught lad again went to see his bride. Although she knew what the boy's mother was up to, she only said, "Take my six-winged horse and go, but don't let the golden apple tree catch you. And on your way back, make sure to stop by my castle first."

The youth straddled the magic stallion, and they soon reached the entrance to the other realm. They let themselves down through a deep hole in the silver vault of this realm, alighting on a meadow of emerald. In the middle of it stood the apple tree, its golden apples sound asleep in the silver moonlight. Gently the boy managed to pick an apple without waking it. Then his steed soared high, making for the hole. But the other golden apples woke up, crying, "Thief!" So the tree shook its branches, and they turned into sinewy golden arms reaching after the robbers. It was too late, though, for the magic horse cleared the silver vault and got beyond their grasp.

Once the lad was back at his bride's castle, she slyly hid his golden apple, giving him another one just like it. Being none the wiser, the queen took the maiden's apple and ate it, saying that she was cured. A week later she pretended to be ill again. This time the monster had told her to ask the boy to fetch spring water from the mountains that keep counsel with the clouds.

Hearing the queen's new request, the girl shook her head and said, "Go, my love, if you must, but this time it won't be so easy. I fear that the clouds will send thunderbolts after you, and the mountains will try to crush you to death with their peaks. Take my twelve-winged stallion and this magic pitcher. Exactly at noontide, the hills and the clouds will keep counsel, leaving their spring unattended. So have the pitcher ready, scoop out the water, and jump into the saddle as fast as you can."

The boy took the pitcher and made for the mountains that keep counsel with the clouds. He waited till the sun rose straight above his head, scooped up the spring water, then leaped into the saddle and fled. But the owners gave chase. The mountains charged like raging bulls, while the clouds sent angry lightning bolts. The twelve-winged stallion swerved and dived and, in the end, managed to get through.

On the way home the lad stopped by his bride's castle, and she secretly exchanged his pitcher for another one. When he gave the girl's water to his mother, the queen, as before, said she felt better. But while the boy was hunting in the forest, the wicked woman went down to the cellar and asked the monster what else she could do to get rid of her son.

"Sit down and play cards with him," said the monster. "But have him play tied up, the way you used to play with his father."

That evening the boy was pleased to see his mother in a cheerful mood. After they ate supper, she said to him, "Do you know, my dear son, what we used to do after meals with your father? We'd play cards with his hands tied."

"If you wish, Mother dear, we can play that way, too," said the unsuspecting son, wanting to please her. The queen brought silk ropes and bound his hands so tightly that the ropes cut into his flesh. Then the boy began to cry, "Mother dear, loosen my ties or I shall die."

"Die then," answered the wicked queen, "for that's what I've wanted all along." Unlocking the cellar, she shouted to her paramour, "Come out, my pigeon, come out and slay him."

Out came the monster, who seized the boy and cut him into tiny pieces. Then he put the pieces into a sack, tied the sack to the boy's horse, and said, "Little horse, carry him dead where you used to carry him alive."

Since the horse would always take the boy to his bride's castle, he took him there this time as well. When the girl saw the ghastly bits of flesh, she started crying, but not for long. Quickly she fitted the bits together and slaughtered the piglet from the earth's edge. Where a part was missing, she replaced it with a piece from the suckling.

Once everything was in its right place, she took the magic water the boy had brought from the spring where the mountains keep counsel with the clouds. As she sprinkled it over him, his joints came together and his body was made whole again. She then dripped juice from the golden apple into the boy's mouth, and behold, he sprang back to life as sound as ever.

The grateful lad kissed his bride and asked her once more to move in with him. "Now I will," replied the smart girl, "but don't you have some unfinished business to attend to first?"

"Thank you for reminding me," said the lad, jumping into the saddle. "I'll be back in no time."

Once home, he took the wicked queen and her monstrous paramour by surprise. He tied both of them to a post, wrapped a reed mat around them, lit a match, and watched them burn to death.

After the lad blew the ashes into the four winds, making sure that nothing was left of the treacherous couple, he rode back to his bride. Soon the young pair had a beautiful wedding, moved into the boy's castle, and lived happily ever after.

— The Stone Statue —

ONCE UPON A TIME there lived a king and queen who had no children. They tried all manner of remedies for this grievous lack, calling physicians, witch doctors, healers, and soothsayers from the four corners of the world, but all to no avail.

One day an old woman came to the palace and sold the queen some herbs. The queen sent the herbs to the kitchen for the cook to make a brew with them. The cook tasted the brew and found it bitter, so she sweetened it with honey, tasted it again, and then brought it to the queen.

Soon thereafter the queen found herself with child, and so did the cook. In due course both the queen and the cook gave birth to two healthy baby boys. The queen named her boy Apple, and the cook named hers Pear.

The two infants grew by leaps and bounds, and soon they turned into strong and handsome youths. They were like two peas in a pod and became sworn brothers. The court was hard put to tell them apart, and the queen passed many a sleepless night over this vexing state of affairs. One day she resolved to put an end to it once and for all. She called her son and branded him with a hot iron.

The prince was so angered that he decided to leave his parents' castle, seeking his fortune abroad. His sworn brother would not stay behind but rode with him.

As they were crossing the border of the kingdom, the two youths came to a bridge where their horses stalled. As they tried to coax the horses forward, out rushed a foul three-headed dragon, blowing fire and smoke through its nostrils. Both youths quickly drew their swords and cut off the dragon's heads. Then they cut out his three tongues and burned the rest, blowing the ashes into the four winds.* After they had strung up the tongues on a stake and stuck it in the ground by the bridge, the sworn brothers rode on.

At dusk they came to a village and knocked on an old woman's door, requesting shelter for the night. Although she was poor, the old woman invited them to supper. Since there was no bread on the table, Prince Apple took out a gold piece and asked her to buy some.

"We have no bread in the village, dear," replied the old woman, "or I'd have put it on the table. For several years now, a monstrous bull with spear-like horns and one wild eye in his forehead has been ravaging our crops. Many a valiant prince has tried to kill him, but none has come out of the encounter alive."

Prince Apple said nothing, but at daybreak he and his sworn brother went together to the field where the bull had made his lair. When the one-eyed monster saw them, he blew fire and smoke through his nostrils and gave a bellow so deep that it shook the earth. Then he pawed the ground, making ready to charge. But the dauntless prince took his bow and shot an arrow right through the monster's eye. Thereupon Pear quickly drew his sword and cut the bull's head off. After they had burned his carcass and blown the ashes into the four winds, the brothers rode on.

Next Apple and Pear came to a land struck by a terrible drought. The riverbeds were dry, and the fields were scorched and strewn all over with dead animals. The people were dressed in mourning and walked about with sad faces. The prince asked an old man where they could get a drink of water.

"Alas, we have no water," said the old man, "for our springs and rivers, which have their sources on the high mountain over there, have been stopped by a giant ogre till our king's daughter agrees to marry him. The king has issued a proclamation that whoever can defeat the ogre will receive his daughter's hand in marriage and half his kingdom. But all who've tried their luck have never returned from the mountain. In despair the princess has now resolved to ease the suffering of her people and deliver herself into the ogre's hands."

When Apple and Pear arrived at the king's palace, the beautiful princess, dressed in mourning, had just mounted her black horse, determined to ride to the ogre's lair. Apple approached the princess and told her she had nothing to fear, for he and his sworn brother would accompany her to the mountain. And at that moment the prince and the princess fell in love.

Hardly had the princess and her champions reached the mountain when a frightful roar shook the forest. The ogre had smelled them and was coming for his prey. But Apple and Pear drew their swords and told the girl to take shelter behind them.

"Out of my way, wretched mortals," snarled the ogre, blowing fire and smoke through his nostrils, "or I'll eat you for supper."

The sworn brothers kept silent and charged, bringing down the ogre, but not before he had dealt a mortal wound to the prince. Pear was about to take the ogre's life when the foul monster said, "If you spare me, I'll release all the springs on the mountain and bring your brother back to life into the bargain."

"How can you do that?" asked Pear.

"Do you see the thunderstruck oak behind that rock? Its hollowed trunk houses a spring with miraculous waters that can make one whole again."

"Release the streams, and then we'll see," said Pear.

The ogre gave out another frightful roar, and behold, all the mountain streams started flowing again. Then Pear asked the princess to fetch some water from the magic spring. They poured a few drops on Apple's lips, and the prince instantly sprang back to life.

"Oh, how I have slept, brother," said Apple.

"And you'd be sleeping still," answered Pear, "had we not awakened you, brother."

After the two youths had slain the ogre, burning his remains and blowing the ashes into the four winds, they took the princess back to her father's palace. Amid great rejoicing, the whole entourage set out

with pomp and ceremony for the land of Apple's parents, where the wedding between the prince and the princess was to take place. The sworn brothers rode ahead of the group to prepare the king and queen for their arrival.

At nightfall Apple and Pear decided to camp under an old yew tree and resume their journey in the morning. But at the stroke of midnight, Pear awoke to a flutter of wings above him. Three turtledoves alighted on the limbs of the yew and began a conversation. Although he understood their language, the cook's son pretended he was none the wiser.

"Sisters dear," cooed one of them, "there lies Prince Apple sound asleep, but he wouldn't sleep so peacefully if he knew that an old ogress, the mother of the three foul beasts he slew, is plotting her revenge. On the morning of his wedding with the king's daughter, a crone will bring the bride a silver wedding gown spun more finely than gossamer. And should the bride wear it, she would perish together with the bridegroom. But he who says a word of this to another soul will turn to stone up to his knees."

"Sisters dear," cooed the second dove, "there sleeps the unsuspecting Prince Apple, who would awaken in a cold sweat if he knew that on his wedding day the nuptial carriage will be drawn by his foe, the old ogress, in the shape of six white horses. And should he and his bride step into it, the ogress would hurl them into the depths of hell. But he who says a word of this to another soul will turn to stone up to his waist."

"Sisters dear," cooed the third dove, "there lies Prince Apple sound asleep, and little does he know that on his wedding night, should her other schemes fail, his foe the old ogress will crawl into his chamber in the shape of a viper and sting him and his bride to death. But he who says a word of this to another soul will turn to stone entirely."

After that the turtledoves flew away. But Pear could not go back to sleep as he pondered how he could best shield his sworn brother from these perils and not turn to stone.

Imagine the joy of the old king and queen, and that of the cook, when they saw their sons return safe and sound. The wedding preparations took several weeks, but finally the appointed day arrived.

Early that morning a crone came knocking on the palace gate. In her arms was a silver wedding gown spun more finely than gossamer as a gift from the fates. But the cook's son was on the lookout. Instantly he drew his sword and cut off the crone's head, throwing it into the fire along with her gift. The bride and the whole court were appalled, not the least because Pear would give no reason for his deed. But the king let it pass, at his son's request.

After the wedding ceremony, just as the newlyweds were coming out of the royal chapel amid the ringing of all the church bells in the village, there came the royal carriage pulled by six splendid white steeds no one had seen before. But to the horror of the wedding party, Pear again drew his sword and quickly cut off the heads of the horses, throwing their trunks to the dogs. The queen, who had never liked the cook's son in the first place, insisted that he be put to death. But the bridegroom's plea on behalf of his sworn brother prevailed once more.

That night, before the newlyweds withdrew to their chamber, Pear hid under the nuptial bed without breathing a word to anyone. Around midnight who should slither in but a deadly viper, ready to dart at the newlyweds blissfully asleep in each other's arms. Out came Pear, sword in hand, cutting the viper in two. He threw it into the fire and left no trace of the evil ogress.

At that very moment the couple awoke and saw Pear with his sword drawn over their heads. Brought before the king and queen, he refused to account for his deed, and the queen accused him of intending to slay the prince and his bride because he was consumed with envy of their happiness. Not knowing what to believe, Apple did not defend his sworn brother as wholeheartedly as he had before. So the king ordered that the cook's son be put to death on the rack.

Seeing that his fate was sealed, Pear asked Apple to summon the whole court because he wished to tell them a story before being put to death. The prince complied with Pear's last request, and the cook's son began:

"Once upon a time, there lived two sworn brothers who were like two peas in a pod, even though one was born the son of a queen, and the other, the son of a cook. The queen resented this uncanny likeness, and branded her son with a hot iron to mark him apart from the cook's son. Angered by her deed, the prince took his sworn brother and went into the wide world. In the course of his journey the valiant prince, aided by the cook's son, rid the world of three foul monsters. When he slew the last one, he also saved from the ogre's clutches a princess, who became the prince's bride. But an evil crone, the mother of the three monsters, plotted the prince's undoing, as the cook's son found out from a conversation among three turtledoves. The first dove said that on their wedding day the old ogress would bring a silver gown as a gift to the bride, and should she wear it, both she and the bridegroom would perish. But, the dove added, he who uttered a word of this to another soul would turn to stone up to his knees."

As soon as Pear finished this part of his story, he turned to stone up to his knees. Apple, the princess, and the cook begged him to say no more, but Pear went on:

"The second dove said that after the wedding ceremony a royal carriage drawn by the old witch in the shape of six white horses would await the newlyweds. And should they step into the carriage, the ogress would hurl them into the depths of hell. But, the dove added, he who uttered a word of this to another soul would turn to stone up to his waist."

No sooner had Pear breathed these words than he changed to stone up to his waist. And despite the tearful entreaties of the whole court, he continued:

"Then the third dove said that on the wedding night the old witch would steal into the nuptial chamber in the shape of a viper, stinging the newlyweds to death. But, the dove added, he who uttered a word of this to another soul would turn to stone entirely."

With those words, Pear changed to stone completely.

Imagine the bitter tears shed by the prince and the princess, to say nothing of the poor cook. Consumed by remorse, Apple had the stone statue of his sworn brother brought into his chamber, where he could gaze at it day and night.

Time went by, and the princess gave birth to a beautiful baby boy who was the spitting image not only of his father, but of the stone statue as well. The baby grew faster than any boy of his age, and he was the apple of his father's eye. On the night of the little boy's third birthday, however, the prince and the princess had the same dream. In the dream an old man appeared before them, saying that if they wanted Pear to come back to life, they must slay their son and sprinkle the stone statue with his blood.

After many consultations with all the priests in the land, the distraught parents took the boy and slit his throat, dousing the statue with his innocent blood. And lo and behold! The stone man came back to life.

"Oh, how I have slept, brother," said Pear.

"And you'd be sleeping still," answered Apple, "had we not awakened you, brother."

When Pear saw the slain body of his nephew, he understood the parents' heartrending sacrifice. Immediately he walked over to the boy, and, touching his little forehead with his hand, brought him back to life. The court was overjoyed with these wondrous events, and the king gave a splendid feast. And they all lived happily and harmoniously ever after.

About the Stories

W E HAVE ANGLICIZED most of the Transylvanian Christian names for the benefit of our North American audience.

Part One: Ghosts, Vampires, and Werewolves

THE WHITE CROSS. This tale is based on an old legend Mihai heard from his great-uncle about an ancient wooden cross outside their mountain hamlet in the western Transylvanian Alps.

The village folk believe that sometimes unhappy people cannot rest in their graves and will haunt the scene of their past misfortunes. In this story Joseph returns as a **zmeu,** a word that has no precise equivalent in English. A *zmeu* can be either an evil spirit, or an evil legendary creature such as an ogre or a ghoul, and has uncanny powers.

THE FOREST. Dezső heard the original version of this tale from some loggers who lived and worked in the thick Carpathian forest of northeastern Transylvania. (The Latin word *Transylvania* means "across, or beyond, the woods," and in the olden times this land was one vast expanse of virgin forest.)

The **spirits of the forest** are of nonhuman origin, but can assume any shape and form, including a human one, and can become visible or invisible at will. Like other Transylvanian nonhuman ghosts, they can be guardian spirits of a place (*genii loci*). They may also guard hollowed trees, mines, treasure sites, and so forth. They hark back to a pre-Christian, pantheistic age when people believed many things were inhabited by supernatural or divine beings. These spirits can be either evil or benign. But even the benign spirits will always punish improper human behavior.

THE BITANG. This story is based on an old tale Dezső heard from his grandfather one winter, when they went into the forest to gather firewood and saw fresh wolf tracks in the snow.

In Transylvanian folk medicine **camomile tea** is believed to have great healing properties.

In some parts of Transylvania, village people believe that the third, seventh, or twelfth son or daughter, if a **bitang** (a child born out of wedlock or as the result of incest), can become a werewolf. An acute feeling of guilt or some other form of mental anguish can trigger this frightful transformation. Once they become adults, these unfortunates are periodically seized by madness, when they run into the wilderness and change into wolves. They can be ferocious, attacking anybody or anything in their way. They suffer from this sad condition only while alive and will not return after death.

THE JEALOUS VAMPIRE. Mihai heard this tale long ago from an old Gypsy who peddled wooden spoons and iron caldrons through the mountain hamlets of western Transylvania. One hot summer afternoon, he stopped by Mihai's cottage and asked him for a mug of cold spring water. He rewarded Mihai with this ancient story, versions of which can be found all over Transylvania.

Vampires are ghosts who have the "evil eye"; they can put a hex on you with their evil look and can feed on fresh human or animal blood. In this tale, Maria temporarily became one of the "living dead" or the "undead." They are a living vampire's dead victims, who can themselves become vampires if they knowingly had dealings with their attacker while alive. As she came under a vampire's spell unknowingly, however, Maria could be rescued by magic. Ultimately, the safety of Maria's soul depended on her not acknowledging the vampire's identity ("I saw nothing") and thus accepting him for what he is.

The removal of a corpse through a **hole in the wall**, rather than through the doorway, is common in the burial rites of many ancient communities. It is meant to ensure the deceased person's well-being in the afterlife or the good luck of surviving relatives.

A **boyar** is a rich Transylvanian landowner, but the boyar in our story obviously has magic powers as well. The practice of tearing the **throbbing heart** out of a witch doctor's chest and employing it for magic purposes is common in many ancient rituals.

SPECIAL DELIVERY. Dezső heard the original version of this tale almost thirty years ago from an old Saxon shoemaker in the village of Zeiden.

The Saxons are a German ethnic group who settled in the rich valleys of southern Transylvania a few hundred years ago. They built numerous castles and fortresses, and each of these has its own legend, if not its own ghost. In this legend a human spirit returns from the grave to fulfill a purpose not fulfilled in life, as in "The White Cross." Although these spirits are scary, they often deserve our compassion rather than our hate or contempt.

Part Two: Haunted Treasures

THE THREE PARTNERS. This gold miner's tale is based on an old story that Mihai heard from his great-aunt Valeria, who used to own a gold mine before Transylvania came under Communist rule. Late at night she would ride into town, carrying saddlebags full of gold ore from her mine in the mountains. She would always travel alone and carry a gun to defend herself against robbers. Aunt Valeria is now ninety-two years old and is still telling marvelous stories to her great-great-grandchildren.

Like other places in the Transylvanian folk imagination, the gold mines are guarded by nonhuman ghosts that can appear at will in any guise they choose. Like other nonhuman spirits (such as those of the forest), the **spirits of the mine** are seldom willful or cruel unless provoked. As a rule they reward good conduct and punish wrongdoing. By acting properly, therefore, mortals can appease, avoid, or reap benefits from these spirits, as the situation demands.

THE GYPSY FIDDLERS. Mihai heard this story one summer when he went to pick mushrooms in the forest with his childhood friends. They came upon a ravine where the villagers believed a treasure was buried, and one of his friends told him the local legend associated with it.

Buried treasures have a well-established place in Transylvanian folklore. People believe that they start burning at midnight on certain days of the year. The ones burning with a yellow flame are as a rule free of ghosts and relatively safe to unearth. The ones burning with a **green flame** are dangerous, for they belong to an evil spirit, or to the human ghost of a previous owner who acquired his treasure in an evil way.

THE FEMALE SNAKE. Mihai was told a variant of this story by his mother, who heard it from some miners from the Abrud region in southwestern Transylvania. It is a typical gold miner's yarn, interwoven with fairy-tale elements. The motif of the female snake goes back to Greek mythology and beyond, where Lamia is a deceitful serpent that attracts mortals under the guise of a beautiful woman. Here, of course, the serpent appears in her positive role, as a cross between a good fairy and a generous mine spirit.

THE SIX-FINGERED HAND. This story comes also from the Abrud region and was told to Mihai in his childhood by his mother.

Almost every Transylvanian village has its colorful local celebrity or "village fool" who, whether he is feared or laughed at, is almost always misunderstood by the other villagers. He is often avoided by his neighbors for no other reason than because he is different. He may be born with a handicap, such as a hump on his back or a lame foot, which is often compensated for by an uncommon gift, such as supernatural strength, or an ability to find gold or foretell the future. In our tale Elijah is more than a village fool. He also has some of the powers of a mine spirit.

THE RED ROSE. Like the two previous stories this tale comes originally from the Abrud region, and Mihai heard it from his mother. The Abrud region is famous for its gold, which can be either panned out of the tricky mountain streams or wrested from the hard mountain rock. The gold here is well known for its reddish color, which is caused by its high copper content. The old man is obviously a benign spirit of the mine.

THE ANCIENT FORTRESS. Mihai heard a version of this tale in a southern Transylvanian village near Deva. There are several ruins of ancient castles and fortresses in that region, and they are believed by the local people to hide enormous treasures.

The legends may have their origins in local history. During times of siege, the noblemen buried their treasures under their castles in order to prevent them from falling into enemy hands. It is believed, for example, that under the ruins of Vlad Dracul's fortress in the Borgo Pass, near the village of Frumuşeaua, there is more gold stashed away than anywhere else in Transylvania.

No treasure can be dug up without the permission of its guardian spirits, but under certain conditions a few chosen mortals can gain access to a treasure for a short time.

Part Three: Eerie Fairy Tales

THE DARK STRANGER. Dezsö heard the original version of this story from an old man in Csikbánkfalva, western Transylvania, some thirty years ago. The plot springs from the worldwide belief that certain people will, out of ignorance or greed, enter into a contract with the forces of evil.

The dark stranger's defeat and the two brothers' resuscitation by means of holy bread underscore the importance of bread in many rural cultures. In rural Transylvania bread is staple fare, enjoying an almost sacred status. To this day, before cutting a fresh loaf of bread, Transylvanian farmers make the sign of the cross over it; they regard wasting bread or throwing it away as a grievous sin. The **mix of black and white flour** used to reconstitute the two brothers represents the Transylvanian popular belief that all human beings are a mixture of good and evil, purity and sin.

This story is also a good example of a blending of Christian and pagan elements. Christian images such as of holy water, communion with the powers of light and darkness, and redemption are fused with ancient images of magic and witchcraft.

THE RED EMPEROR'S SON. Mihai heard a variant of this fairy tale from an old woman at a *clacă*, a gathering of villagers to help a neighbor with a seasonal task, such as making hay or reaping the grain before the rainy season. The neighbor organizing the *clacă* is responsible for the food, drink, and entertainment of his helpers. Sometimes Gypsy musicians are brought to play during the *clacă*, or old folks are asked to tell stories.

Our tale borrows elements from Transylvanian vampire lore. The terrifying ending underscores the fact that in Transylvanian folklore the forces of darkness are often triumphant.

THE WHEEL OF FIRE. Dezső heard this fairy tale in his childhood from his father. It follows the popular belief that some tormented souls cannot depart from this world even after their bodies are properly buried. They will often take the shape of animals such as black cats, dogs, and bats, or of inanimate objects such as wheels, pitchforks, poles, and so forth. The motif of good and evil twins is widespread in European fairy tales, but here it is creatively combined with that of disobedient children.

THE WICKED QUEEN. The original version of this story was told to Mihai by an old woman from a Saxon village near Brasov, in southeastern Transylvania. It is most likely of German origin, but many variants exist in the folklore of other Transylvanian ethnic groups as well. One of its best-known European versions is the story of Red Pea Boy.

This tale is a typical Transylvanian variation on the widely known motif of the evil stepmother or evil mother-in-law, interlaced with the equally well-known motifs of the heroic quest and of white and black magic present in medieval romances.

THE STONE STATUE. Mihai heard a variant of this story in his childhood while waiting for his turn at the water mill. The mill is an ideal place for storytelling because people have to wait in line to have their grain ground, and so they while away the time trading stories.

Versions of this fairy tale can be found not only in Transylvania but also throughout central and southern Europe. All of the enemies Apple and Pear must do battle with belong to the *zmeu* category, so they must be eliminated in a ritualistic manner, by cutting off their heads, burning their remains, and **blowing the ashes into the four winds**.

Further Reading

To the best of our knowledge, there are no other collections of Transylvanian tales available in English in this country. Readers who are interested in finding out more about the ethnographic and historical background of our stories may consult the following:

MacKenzie, Andrew. *Dracula Country: Travels and Folk Beliefs in Romania*. London: Barker, 1977.

McNally, Raymond, and Radu Florescu. *In Search of Dracula: A True History of Dracula and Vampire Legends*. Greenwich, Connecticut: N.Y. Graphic Society, 1972.

Pascu, Ştefan. *A History of Transylvania*. Detroit, Michigan: Wayne State University, 1982.

Senn, Harry A. *Were-wolf and Vampire in Romania*. Boulder and New York: University of Colorado, 1982.

Readers interested in Romanian-, Hungarian-, German-, and Romany-language source materials can contact us through our publisher. The following books may interest the general reader, since these books also feature spooky stories grounded in one or more folk traditions:

Brown, Roberta. *The Walking Tree and Other Scary Stories*. Little Rock, Arkansas: August House, 1991.

Leach, Maria. *The Thing at the Foot of the Bed*. New York: Philomel, 1987.

———. *Whistle in the Graveyard: Folktales to Chill Your Bones*. New York: Viking, 1974.

Lyons, Mary E. *Raw Head, Bloody Bones: African American Tales of the Supernatural*. New York: Scribner's, 1991.

McKissack, Patricia. *The Dark-Thirty: Southern Tales of the Supernatural*. New York: Alfred A. Knopf, 1992.

San Souci, Robert, and Katherine Coville. *Short and Shivery: Thirty Chilling Tales*. New York: Doubleday, 1987. An international selection.

Schwartz, Alvin. *Scary Tales to Tell in the Dark*. New York: HarperCollins, 1981. From American folklore. There are two companion volumes: all three have excellent bibliographies for further research.

Schwartz, Howard. *Lilith's Cave: Jewish Tales of the Supernatural*. New York: Oxford University Press, 1991.